CROWN OF BLOOD

Book Two - Crown of Death Saga

KEARY TAYLOR

Taylor, Keary, 1987-
Crown of Blood (Crown of Death) : a novel / by Keary Taylor. – 1st ed.

ALSO BY KEARY TAYLOR

~

BLOOD DESCENDANTS UNIVERSE

THE FALL OF ANGELS TRILOGY

THREE HEART ECHO

THE EDEN TRILOGY

THE McCAIN SAGA

WHAT I DIDN'T SAY

CHAPTER 1

EIGHT TIMES NOW, MY EYES HAVE OPENED, NEWLY transformed into a brilliant, violent red. Twice, at the castle. Once, in the bedroom of a palace in the desert. Once, on the lawn beneath the moon. Once, in the middle of a ballroom. Once, in a breezy seaside home. And once, under the dirt in the jungle outskirts.

But always, the fire races up my throat as my eyes slide open. And this time, the name...the name I have searched for through time and the dark whispers out over my lips.

Beat, beat, beat.

Contract, expand.

Burn, burn, burn.

Warm highways, pushing gushing liquid beneath her beautiful skin.

In one swift and utterly smooth movement, I rise from the bed and grip the woman's shoulders. There it is: the old, old as time, familiar sensation of my fangs lengthening, followed by the pooling of toxins in my mouth.

I'm sure she is terrified. But she doesn't move. Doesn't scream.

And I don't care.

My fangs sink into her neck and as soon as I pull, she's utterly still.

I draw in her blood. It rushes over my tongue. Down my throat. It pools in my belly. But it's not enough. It's never enough the first time to cool the burning inside of me.

So I suck harder. I draw it out of her.

Every.

Drop.

Slowly, the woman begins to grow limp in my arms. Slowly, her body begins to collapse. My hands wrap around her waist, easily supporting her weight, holding her tight as I continue to drink.

She grows lighter, and I grow heavier.

As the flow begins to slow, I feel my burning body begin to cool. The flames stop licking up my legs. Acid stops racing through my arms. The heat in my throat cools from a raging inferno to a dull burn.

Finally, as I pull the last drop, the heat is extinguished.

A contented sigh crosses my lips as I release the woman and let her exsanguinated body collapse to the ground.

Two people react inside of me—the one that feels the most familiar, the one I know I am, and the one who feels so far away, but rooted in my heart.

One is horrified. One screams that I've just killed a woman, that I did that.

The other regrets it, but knows it is only part of the circle of life.

Motion to my left pulls my attention.

And everything in me stills. Goes hot and cold at the same time. Falls backward through thousands of years and bounces off the moments just before my death.

Cyrus slowly steps forward, his eyes wide, his mouth slightly slack. Hope, fear, they're both there in equal measures in his eyes.

"What did you just say?" he breathes, his eyes wide and fixed on my face.

I stand frozen, rooted, staring back at him. A violent storm rages through me, roaring with wind and rain and sand.

Emotion rises in me and it pricks the back of my eyes.

Finally, after all this time.

"I beg of you," Cyrus whispers as he comes to a stop, just two feet in front of me. "Please tell me what you just said."

He's poised. Every muscle in his body is on edge. Ready to rush forward. Ready to rage in disappointment. Ready to tear this entire world down.

He can do it.

I know he can.

He can do anything.

A single tear pushes out onto my cheek, silently slipping down my face.

Slowly, Cyrus raises his hands to my face, placing one on each cheek. With his thumb, he brushes my tear away.

"What did you just say?" he whispers again, so quiet, that just four days ago, I would not have been able to hear his words.

KEARY TAYLOR

I squeeze my eyes closed for just a moment, forcing out more tears. I take one breath, searching inside of me.

No. Please no, I offer up a silent prayer.

But I can't deny the truth.

I know the truth.

I know exactly who I am.

"Sevan," I say, with my voice clear as day.

Cyrus' eyes widen, and his breathing stops. Crystal clear, so transparent I can see right down to his heart.

"I never once said that name to Logan," he says, his voice holding a quiver. "I commanded that no other breathe it, either." I see the desperation clawing its way to the surface. "Logan never knew that name."

All of my insides tremble.

I'm going to fall apart.

I shake my head. "No," I breathe. "You never told me." I raise my hand, lacing my fingers into his hair, cupping around the back of his head. "But I remember, *im yndmisht srtov*."

He takes a shaky, short intake of breath as his eyes fill with tears. "Sevan," he breathes. And neither he, nor I, in some parts of me, can stand the separation any longer. His arms wrap around me, pulling us together, crushing our hearts together.

"Sevan," he breathes, over and over. "Sevan, *im yndmisht srtov*."

Sevan, *my forever heart*.

Spoken in our original tongue, the language we both spoke at one time. A time when I was just a girl, and he, a boy.

4

"All this time," Cyrus breathes. "So many years. Too many centuries."

His voice cracks, and his words come out mixed with sobs and cries.

He releases me, once more looking into my eyes as he places his hands on either side of my face. His own is red, tears staining his cheeks, his eyes bloodshot with emotion. But he smiles. Bigger and wider and more genuinely real than I've ever seen as Logan Pierce.

I feel emotions rip inside of me. My heart can't handle the two parts of me that truly are one.

The love in his eyes. The devotion I feel in his very hands. The relief in his shoulders.

For a woman I was not for the past twenty years.

"I pray a thousand prayers of gratitude," Cyrus says as his eyes study mine and I witness his absolute joy. "For the days we have right now, for the uncertainty we don't have to endure over the next few weeks. Never," he shakes his head, still smiling wide. "Never before has it all come back to you in the very moment of Resurrection."

He lets out a relieved sigh, still so overjoyed.

And he leans forward, his eyes beginning to slide closed.

I take a step back before he can kiss me, stepping out of his grasp.

His eyes fly open, confusion filling them as they return to me.

"Sevan," he says, his brows furrowing. "What is it? What's wrong?"

Once more, tears fill my eyes. I shake my head, taking another step back, away from him. "I know..." I struggle to form the words, to get a grasp on my identity. "Please, don't call me that. Not…not yet."

His expression slackens slightly and I see the confusion and searching behind his eyes. He doubts. Maybe I'm not Sevan. But there's no way I could have known her name if I wasn't. There is no way I would have known our name for one another from thousands of years ago if I wasn't.

"It's alright," he says, swallowing once. "I'm sorry, Lo…" He takes one breath, struggling over the word. For just a moment, his eyes fall away. And I understand. After all this time, I deny it of him. "I'm sorry, Logan."

Tears fall from my eyes, and I can't stop them. I shake my head as I take one step away. "It's not alright," I say as I continue shaking my head. "I am so tired, Cyrus. Over and over and over again this happens, and over and over we have played this moment. But still, no matter how happy we might be for a time, no matter how we try to change ourselves to reverse what you did, we know the fate coming for us. For me."

I turn, bracing my hands on the dresser along the wall, letting my head fall between my shoulders.

I cry.

I cry as Logan. I cry as Sevan.

I cry as a broken woman.

I hear his footsteps as he slowly walks over the carpet. His hands warm my arms as he places them on me. One of his hands slides up, cupping around my shoulder as his other slithers around my waist and his body molds to mine from behind, cradling me against him.

"We will find a way to fix it this time," he whispers against my ear. His voice is so full of tenderness. It bears the weight of a billion promises. "Times are changing. There are whisperings. We will end the curse this time. I swear it to you, my love. I will fix what I did."

"How, Cyrus?" I demand as I yank away from the dresser, out of his grasp. "Over and over you say this, making me promises. And I always believe them. And over and over, I starve. I wither. Over and over, I die a slow death while watching you cry and make more promises. You have had all this time, Cyrus, and still I die. Do not make me promises you cannot keep. Even you are not stronger than the universe who saw fit to punish you."

We stand across the room from one another, staring, breathing hard.

Shock and hurt are written all over his face.

Logan is satisfied, pleased that I've put this man in his place, told it to him as was true. But she also can't stand the sadness that's growing in his eyes. She wants to wrap her arms around him and tell him that it's all right.

Sevan is just so tired. So cracked and time worn. As much as she wants to smile and wrap her arms around her husband, she's just so tired.

"I…" Cyrus begins to say, but his hands fall to his side. He doesn't have the words.

"You don't know what it's like, to have to Resurrect. The pain you experience in those four days of lying there, dead. The horror of making your first kill," I extend my hand to the dead woman lying on the floor. "The confusion of having to adjust to a new state of being. Over and over and over again, Cyrus. I have died *eight* deaths. And had to go through the pain of opening my eyes again to a new life *eight* times."

Cyrus' brows furrow, his expression unsure. "Seven."

My brows furrow, as well. "What?"

He takes one step forward. "Seven. You have died seven deaths. And now Resurrected seven times."

I search, thinking back through the past. Looking through each life.

But even though I know they are there, I can't see through all the fog in my brain.

I may have remembered who I was immediately, but the details of my past lives have not come into focus yet.

I shake my head as tears once more come to my eyes. "Eight," I say again, feeling sure of it.

Cyrus walks forward and reaches out to take my hand. He raises it to his lips, pressing them to my knuckles. "I cannot change the past, and you're right. I cannot make promises about the future. But, Sev..." He closes his eyes for a moment, taking in a breath. "Logan. I can only be a man in this moment. A man who is overjoyed, overcome with gratitude that after all this time, we are together again."

I crack.

Splinter.

It's all I wanted the past few weeks. To be held by Cyrus. To have him whisper in my ear. To have his hands on me. To know what it feels like to have his lips on mine.

But in this moment, I am consumed by pain.

I pull my hand out of his. I take another step back, away from him.

"I need to be alone," I say quietly.

He looks at me, confusion and hurt in his eyes. "Logan..."

"Damn it, Cyrus!" I bellow. "I need a few moments to get it together!"

They were Logan's words, and Sevan's boldness.

Eyes wide, he takes one step back. He hesitates for four long seconds. But finally, he steps to the side. Never looking away from me, he steps around me, opens the door, and after another moment of hesitation, closes it behind him.

I stand there, breathing hard. The moment Cyrus is out of sight, the tears come. But they're quiet tears. I don't cry, don't sob, just let them roll furiously down my face.

I look around the room. It's the same room I've lived in for the past month. Those are my things on the desk. My shoes lined up behind the door. Those are my clothes hanging in the closet.

I walk to the bathroom and slowly step in front of the mirror.

Dark brown hair hangs most of the way down my back. A strong jawline and a balanced nose make my face appealing. Green-yellowish eyes mark them as unique.

My hands rise up to my face, touching it.

It's the face I've had for my entire life, but a face that doesn't even look familiar.

No more is my hair naturally curly. No more are my eyes dark. No more is there a scar on my left cheek. No longer am I as tall as the man who stands just on the other side of my bedroom door.

I've worn nine different faces over two millennia.

Which is the real one?
Who the hell am I?
Logan Pierce? Or Sevan?

CHAPTER 2

I Resurrected around six in the evening.

I take a shower at seven.

At eight I dare go to the blackout curtains that cover my bedroom window and peek outside. Only to slam them shut. It's only twilight, the sun has long since sunk below the horizon. But even that minimal light is enough to make my eyes burn with incredible pain.

At nine, I lie on my bed, staring up at the ceiling.

Thousands of thoughts are racing through my head. One event after another that has happened, is happening, or will need to happen in the very near future.

I died four days ago because I leapt in front of a stake meant for Cyrus. A spy infiltrated this house, intent on killing Cyrus. Just days before that, they ransacked the house. They looked for evidence that the King was indeed here in Greendale, Colorado.

Cyrus has had thousands of enemies over the centuries.

As I think back, I know there have been countless attempts on his life. None of them successful.

I look toward the door, to where the hall is. To where Cyrus killed the man who ended my life.

Maybe this individual acted alone. Maybe not. Maybe this isn't over.

I look back up at the ceiling. I'm not ready. I'm not ready to jump back into this life, these deadly games.

So I turn to something more familiar.

Rath.

I search, trying to find that name in the past. To recall any previously forgotten knowledge about him, but there isn't anything. Nothing at all.

But Logan knows exactly where he is. I know what needs to happen now. He was to remain in the House of Valdez' custody until I died.

It's time for his release.

I let my mind wander, trailing from one thought to the next.

The betrayal I felt as Rath told me the truth about why he came into my life. The coldness of his cell. The strength of Edmond Valdez and the words he spoke to me. The hints at my birth mother.

I think of the gladiator game Cyrus made them play as punishment.

Punishment for the show they created for him.

Punishment for thinking Sevan…my story, would serve as entertainment.

The look in Cyrus' eyes fills my vision. The brokenness I witnessed in his eyes. The way his hands fisted. The pain of centuries in his gaze. The sob that ripped from his throat when I left him to grieve.

I raise my hands to my chest, holding in the pain I felt for him then.

I may be two people right now, trying to figure out how to be one.

But in this moment, I'm Logan Pierce.

I'm that woman who read his pain. The one who dared speak out against a House of immortal vampires to end the tale that gave the man I love so much pain.

A breath of agony sucks into my chest suddenly. I bite my lower lip to hold in the cry of anguish and pain and longing.

I sit up in the bed and look over at the clock.

11:21.

Please, Logan, Cyrus begged me as he caressed my arm, my body. *Don't make me wait.*

Guilty? I had asked him.

The guilt of feeling as if I am betraying my wife, he had whispered to me as I lay there dying. *Because when I look at you, Logan...*

My hand pulls the door to my bedroom open.

It never ceases to amaze me, every time I Resurrect, just how truly incredible being a vampire is. The absolute sense of balance. The feeling of strength and power that flows through my veins. The perfect clarity of vision. And the crystal clear hearing.

Cyrus is in his bedroom.

I hesitate with my hand on his doorknob for just a moment. I'm a shaking, trembling mess. It's incredible that emotions can even outweigh my vampiric abilities. Can bring me to my knees.

In this moment, I let go of the past.

In this moment, I close off Sevan. And I'm just Logan Pierce.

I twist the doorknob and push the door open.

It's dark, but I can see clearly.

He stands beside the window, looking out over the property. But he looks over his shoulder at me, his eyes waiting.

I let my own wander over him. He wears a pair of jeans. His feet are bare. A gray t-shirt hugs his form nicely.

I push her away. The woman who knows every inch of this man. Who has touched every surface of his body.

I don't want to be in this moment with her experience in my head.

Right now, I just want to be Logan.

Cyrus stares at me, waiting for my cues. But I see it in his eyes, the burning. The embers. The desire—for a lot of things.

I step inside and close the door behind me.

Slowly, I cross the room through the dark. One step at a time I approach Cyrus, holding his eyes the entire time.

He's silent, but his eyes say a million words. They run up and down me as I cross the space. I wear an oversized shirt that falls halfway to my knees. His eyes take in my legs. Linger on my shoulder where the neck of the shirt has slid off.

I stop just inches from him and let my eyes fall to the space between us. I reach for his hand and lace my fingers into his.

"We may have pretended for a few weeks," I say quietly. My heart is racing, my blood surging through all the feminine parts in me. "Put on a show. But in the end, it was real for me. It did things to me."

"The past few weeks-"

"Please don't say anything," I say, cutting him off. My eyes wander over him, taking every bit of him in, but never quite meet his eyes. "Please just let me have this." I pull our hands up, resting them against my chest. "For just this night, please just be with me."

I know he can feel it, my heart thundering inside of my rib cage. The sensation of his skin, his hand against my chest, it's overwhelming. I crave his touch. After the past few weeks of longing, of imagining, of fantasizing what it would be like to be touched by Cyrus, here I am.

I asked him not to speak, so he doesn't.

Instead, he wraps his hand around my waist. He draws me in close and he wraps his other hand behind my neck.

I let my eyes slide closed. I wrap my arms around the man who has done such complicated things to my heart. I run my hands up his back, appreciating every muscle on his body.

His breath warms my neck as it comes out in a big sigh. It sends a wave of goose bumps across my skin and I let my head fall backward as a little sound escapes between my lips.

It's just a slight brush at first, his bottom lip against my collarbone. So soft I can't even feel him, only his warmth. But then it happens again, and once more. He shifts, and soon his lips are pressed to the side of my neck, slowly working their way up to the hollow beneath my ear.

I let my hands fall, slowly sliding down, tracing along Cyrus' sides, until they catch on his belt. Through the dark, my fingers search, until they find the hem of his shirt. They slide under the fabric, and my breath catches when they come in contact with flesh.

A needy groan escapes Cyrus' mouth when I touch him and the frenzy in me doubles.

I've fantasized about this dozens of times over these past few weeks. Wondered what my view would be with his shirt removed. Wondered how he would feel. Wondered how he would smell from this close. Wondered what kinds of sounds I could make him make.

His hand slides down, dips dangerously low on my back.

I continue letting my hands slide up.

Over his stomach. Over rises and falls.

Up over his chest muscles.

And it's not enough.

In a swift motion, I pull further up, and Cyrus raises his arms, letting me remove his shirt entirely.

I place one hand on his chest, the other slowly sliding up his arm, appreciating his sculpted body.

Possessively, his hands grip the fabric at my hips and pulls mine to his. His lips come to my jaw, moving up. My entire body ignites with electric sparks when he gently pulls at my earlobe with his teeth.

I moan, utterly satisfied and craving a million degrees more of his touch.

His grip on my hips tightens and I rise up onto my toes. As if I weighed nothing at all, he lifts me, spinning in one motion. He pins me against the wall, his hips holding me in place, pressing hard into me.

His eyes hold a dim glow of red, but I can tell, mine are brilliant and bright. I can't hold anything back right now. Can't think straight to do so in the moment.

My hands return to his chest, relishing in the feeling of my skin against his.

Cyrus takes the hem of my shirt and in one swift motion, pulls it up and over my head and lets it fall to the floor at his feet.

His mouth once more returns to the hollow at the base of my throat and my head falls back against the wall. My hands rise up, fisting in his hair. My fingers lace through its thickness.

Another fantasy fulfilled tonight.

His hands caress my back, rising up, his fingers splayed, as if trying to gain every inch of contact possible. I arch into him, needing more. Craving more of him.

"Logan," he breathes against my flesh.

And a wave crashes down on top of me, drowning me.

My hands come to either side of his face and his eyes meet mine.

Longing. Lust. Desire.

And I want it to be there. Maybe it is, but I'm too scared it isn't real:

Love.

"Say it again," I beg him.

He watches me for a moment, and I know he has to be overanalyzing my request.

But the heat does not diminish in his eyes.

His grip on me tightens, and he steps away from the wall. My legs stay wrapped around his waist and he carries us to the bed in the middle of the room.

Gently he lays me down on it, hovering just above me, his eyes locked on mine. His hands come to my hips, and slowly the right one trails down. His eyes wander. To my stomach. To the black panties I wear. Up, over the bra I wear, over the rise of my breasts.

He dips, pressing his lips to my stomach. "Logan," he whispers against my flesh.

Once more, my hands come to fist in his hair. I arch against the bed, anxious and eager for his touch.

"Logan," he says again. His eyes slide closed and he draws my knee up, holding it against his side.

My eyes flutter closed and every cell in my body is focused on the sensation of his hands exploring my body.

I love you. The words echo in my brain.

But there are too many sides to this. Too many complicated aspects. And the words cannot come past my lips. Not yet.

For now, I can just touch him. I can just exist in this moment, being with Cyrus. Finally.

Finally.

Me and Cyrus. Together.

CHAPTER 3

I DON'T SLEEP. BUT EVENTUALLY I TURN ON MY SIDE, looking out the window. Cyrus curls up behind me, an arm wrapped possessively around my waist. Slowly he breathes against the back of my neck.

He never says anything, as I asked. But we lie there for hours, just existing.

I don't let him kiss me. He never tried. I have no doubt he was thinking about earlier when I backed away from him. He's very much going off of my cues. I never try to kiss him directly on the lips. I need to be at peace with both of my selves before I can do that.

And we don't have sex. There was endless touching. His hands on me, mine all over him. Lips on skin and bodies tangled together. But not sex.

That part is complicated. Again, I need to be at peace with every part of myself. But I've also never taken that step. I've never been with anyone like that.

Around six in the morning, Cyrus presses a gentle kiss to the back of my neck and rolls out of bed. I watch him walk to the closet. He grabs a button-up shirt and he stands in the doorway, watching me as he buttons it up, slowly.

"Good morning," he says quietly as he leans against the doorway, sliding his hands into his back pockets.

I don't say anything. Maybe I manage a small smile. But I'm mostly just watching him.

I see the weight in his expression as he walks forward. He takes my hand and raises it, pressing a kiss to the back of my knuckles. "I'm sure you are thirsty again," he says quietly. "I'll bring you something to drink and ask Fredrick to make breakfast."

I wasn't. I hadn't thought about my thirst, but the moment he says it, my throat is burning.

I swallow once, and nod.

He crosses the room and walks out, swinging the door partially closed.

I roll onto my back and stare up at the ceiling.

Last night was everything I dreamed it would be. Finally touching Cyrus and having him touch me filled a hole I'd recently discovered I had in my chest. Letting him press his lips to nearly every part of my body was the most blissful experience of my life.

But I'd also made a deal with myself.

Just one night.

Just something to hold onto.

Until I figure everything out.

I get up and go change. Comfortable, casual clothes. I braid my hair to the side. Put on some make up.

I look at myself in the mirror just once, before heading out the door.

"How soon can the pilot be ready to depart?"

I hesitate at the top of the stairs when I hear Cyrus' voice.

"He said he will be ready whenever you are," Fredrick answers in his heavy accent.

"Excellent," Cyrus says. I hear him bite into something and chew. "After breakfast, I need you and Mina to pack our things and we'll be off. I am very anxious to return home and return to our life."

Crack.

I raise a hand to my chest.

Our life.

I look around, as if searching for answers, to clear solutions, and clear thoughts. But they're nowhere to be found.

What I know is waiting for me in Roter Himmel, in Austria, doesn't feel like *our* life.

I swallow once, and descend the stairs.

I can hear his racing heart before I even turn the stairs. Can smell the sweat on his palms.

And I feel ill for a second. I feel so disgusted with what I am, that this is because of me.

But the moment I see the man, sitting at the dining chair, his hands tied to the arms, a gag in his mouth, I see his pulse in his neck. I can't think of anything other than the burning inferno in my throat.

His eyes only widen for a moment as I stand across the great room one moment, and am sinking my fangs into his neck the next. A little muffled scream penetrates my ears for just a second before he grows quiet and limp.

I suck his blood.

I pull it out of his body.

It slips down my throat.

It curls its way into my body.

It hits my stomach with satisfaction.

I moan as I take another pull, cupping him tightly to me so he doesn't slump in the chair.

One more deep pull, and I release him.

I straighten and wipe the drip of his blood that escaped onto my lip.

The man sways, his eyes heavy, hardly able to stay open.

Cyrus steps forward. And suddenly, with a sharp twist, he snaps the man's neck.

"Cyrus!" I bellow, stepping forward. But it's too late. The man falls limply, his head and chest hitting the wooden tabletop. "What...why?"

"You took most, but not all of his blood," Cyrus says as he walks back to the counter where Fredrick is preparing the food. I hardly even realize he's looking at me with big, wide eyes. He even takes a big bow, muttering "my Queen." But my shock, my rage, makes the man invisible. "He would have turned," Cyrus says evenly.

I look back at the dead man. "Into...into a Bitten."

Logan places a hint of a question in it. But Sevan knows the truth. Has seen it happen over and over and over again.

"Yes," Cyrus confirms. "It's been a recent change. That the creation of any Bitten is outlawed, and punishable by death."

My eyes snap to Cyrus in surprise, but Logan has heard it before. I didn't really understand it then. But now, knowing what I do remember, it's a huge development. "Any and all Bitten? Any accidents? Always?"

Cyrus nods. He dishes up a plate and extends it in my direction. "Things have happened recently. It became necessary to eradicate their kind."

"They're *all* dead?" I gape in horror. "Every Bitten, no matter if they were created by accident?"

Cyrus jaw tightens. He sets my plate down on the table. Hard.

"You have not been here for centuries, Sevan," he says in a hard tone. "You do not know what they have done in the past two decades!"

I go cold. I stand a little straighter. My fingers curl into fists.

"I told you not to call me that," I say quietly.

And Cyrus knows he's pushed things too far, gotten too hot too fast. He looks up at me with knowing eyes. But he doesn't say anything.

I walk to the table and place my hands on it. I take a moment, because I know as soon as I say the words, I can never take them back, or undo the consequences of them.

"I'm not going back to Roter Himmel with you," I say, looking up, and finding his forest green eyes.

One beat. Two.

"What?" he says.

I lean further into the table for a moment, gathering my strength. "This isn't simple, Cyrus. It never is."

"I know the adjustment is always hard for you, Sev…" he stops himself from saying the name. "Adjusting to multiple lives, reconciling the past and the present and the even deeper past. But doing it apart can do no good."

He steps forward and I see desperation rising in his eyes. He stops at my side and I see he wants to touch me, to pull me to him. But he doesn't dare.

I stand, facing him.

"Doing it apart is the only way I can do it," I say, absolutely calm. Completely even. "Because right now, inside, I am too complicated. Looking at you is too hard. I have to figure some things out, Cyrus. And I cannot do it with you..." I don't know how to finish the sentence, because there are too many aspects to it.

"I need some time on my own," I say finally.

I knew my words would hurt Cyrus. They would crack him. In my past lives, others have told me stories, given accounts of what Cyrus is like when I am...not with him. He goes mad. He slips into the dark. He does bad things.

So me asking for separation, after what has been 286 years? That feels like a betrayal.

"Go back to Roter Himmel," I say, making my voice soft. "I will return when I am ready."

"Sevan," he whispers. And the name just breaks me further.

I shake my head. And I turn to walk away.

"Where will you go?" he asks. His voice is broken.

I turn back. "I have one item of unfinished business to take care of. The final chip to our bargain."

"Rath," he says, immediately understanding.

I nod. "I'm going back to Las Vegas. You can go home,

and their security can go back with me. I'll be well protected with them."

He hesitates, and he's at an absolute loss for words.

So I take advantage of the moment, when he's not arguing with me. I turn, and walk back to my bedroom to get ready.

~

THERE ARE A MILLION THINGS THAT I DON'T KNOW. DON'T know how to plan for.

I pack nearly every item of clothing I own. I slip the credit card Cyrus gave me weeks ago into my back pocket.

I stand in the middle of my room, looking down at my phone.

"Fredrick," I say without raising my voice.

A second and a half later, there's a light knock on my door and it cracks open. A very timid and frightened looking Fredrick looks in at me.

"Yes, my queen?" he says in German.

I understand him. Because I've spoken the language for over a thousand years, in all its variations. As well as dozens of others.

"I need you to get me some kind of House...directory," I say, looking down at my phone again. "I assume you have such a thing."

Hesitantly, he steps inside. "Yes, your Majesty," he says as he pulls his own cell phone out. He taps a few things on the screen and indicates for me to hold my phone up. A moment later a notification comes through, and I open it to find dozens of names and numbers.

"Thank you," I say, offering him a small smile.

He only bows his head once, and leaves the room.

I scroll through my phone, looking at the names.

House of Himura.

House of Dorian.

House of Martials.

House of Sidra.

House of Conrath.

I stare at the last name for a long time.

For the past twenty years of my life, I have wondered. What my birth parents were like. Who I looked like more. Where they were.

And now I could tap that screen right now, and in a few seconds I could speak to the woman who gave birth to me.

I turn the screen off, and look around, my heart racing.

Not yet.

Someday.

But not today.

I grab my bag, and walk down the stairs.

The house is in a state of calming chaos. Those from the House of Valdez that came here as security are now standing around, waiting to depart. Mina walks in and out of the house, wearing those special sunglasses, carrying bags. Fredrick paces back and forth, speaking on the phone.

But Cyrus stands by the front door.

I very nearly can't handle the pain in his eyes when I look at him. It nearly breaks me, makes me say I'll go with him, return to our home.

But I can't.

He watches me as I walk across the foyer toward him, my bag in hand. He looks me up and down, his gaze so penetrating I nearly feel relieved. Surely he can see down to my heart and understand why I must do what I am doing.

But that pain. It tells me he doesn't.

"Why?" he asks when I stop before him.

"Do you not understand? Even a little?" I ask, begging him to try. I set my bag down, looking up into his eyes.

His lip trembles. His nostrils flare just slightly. His hands are rolled into fists.

"Please," he says. His voice quivers. "Just come home with me. I swear I will make it all better."

Splinter.

He breaks me. Fractures me.

I'm a ruin because of this man.

"No," I say, my voice a hoarse whisper. "Not yet."

He reaches for my hand, bringing my knuckles to his lips. A single tear drips onto my skin as he kisses it. "You *will* come back though?"

He looks up into my eyes for the truthful answer.

"I promise." And my defense crumbles slightly as I take another half a step forward. I place a hand on his cheek. "I promise, *im yndmisht srtov.*"

He squeezes his eyes shut, forcing out another tear. He presses his lips to my palm and then lets it go, standing straight.

"I shall return home and wait then," he says, gathering himself. "We will do our best to keep things quiet, but I suspect it won't be long before the entire world knows of

your return. Until then, if you need anything, please..."
There's that look in his eyes. The one that says he will turn
the world inside out for me. And it makes this even harder.
"Until then, this house is yours to use as you need. Everything in it is yours."

I offer him a sad little smile. "Thank you," I say. "Be
safe, Cyrus."

He just stares at me, and I hate knowing how much pain I
am causing him right now.

So I stoop, picking up my bag. The members of the
House of Valdez scramble forward, taking it from me.

And I can't look back as I walk out the front door after
slipping on my sunshades. Because if I do, I won't really be
able to leave.

The guards load my bag into Cyrus' black sports car. I
pull the keys out of my purse and watch as the guards load
into their own vehicles. I drop into the drivers seat and start
the engine.

Backing out, I make myself not look at the front door
where I know Cyrus is watching. I point the nose of the car
down the driveway and pull out to the main road.

Using voice commands, I set the navigation to the Metro-
Cosmo in Las Vegas. Through the Colorado heat, I start on
my way to Nevada.

I never would have texted or called while driving as a
human. But my vampire senses could drive this car all the
way to Vegas and not have to look at the road. So with my
eyes on my phone, I scroll through the directory Fredrick
sent me. I stop when I see House O'Rourke and hit call.

It rings five times before someone answers.

"Siobhan," I say, goose bumps flashing over my arms. In some ways sliding back into my old life is like swimming through tar. In others, it's like putting on a familiar old sweater. "It's Sevan. I need to talk to Larkin."

I'm met with silence for a very long moment. I consider explaining. Telling her where I am. But Cyrus is right: we do need to be careful. I've been in these politics long enough to know it isn't wise to go spouting my whereabouts to every Royal in the world.

"Give me just a minute to find him," she squeaks out.

Indeed, a minute later, I hear the sound of the phone rustling. And then a deep, smooth voice comes through from around the world.

"Is it true?" he says.

"Yes," I say over the speakerphone. "Just twenty-four hours ago. I need your help."

I can imagine him. The serious look on his dark face. The danger in his eyes. "Anything, my queen."

My skin tingles at his address. "I need you to meet me at the House of Valdez in eleven hours. Can you make it?"

This is where Sevan and Logan clash. Because one side of my brain thinks the request is absolutely ludicrous. Larkin is with the House O'Rourke, in Ireland. Last time I walked the earth, it would have taken weeks of sailing across the ocean and then a transcontinental trek to reach me in Las Vegas.

But Logan has flown thousands of miles. She knows how fast Cyrus reached Greendale just a month ago from Austria.

"Give me twelve and I will be there," Larkin says.

"Done," I say. "I'll see you soon."

CHAPTER 4

THE FEELING OF HIS HANDS ON MY SHOULDERS WAS THE FIRST thing that felt familiar. The warmth of them. The size. The strength held in their grasp. And the edge of danger I felt from them.

"Take your pick," he had whispered in my ear.

Warily, I looked over my shoulder at his face.

For years—my whole life—I had known this day was coming. It had been planned, scheduled to occur on my eighteenth birthday. And now, four days later, here I stood, just sixty seconds after finally rising from the acid of Resurrection and opening my eyes.

"You can take any of them," the King breathed in my ear.

Instantly the hunger was controlling, and I rushed forward, to the line of humans in the great ballroom. The woman's eyes widened a bit, a moment of fear before she met her end as my fangs sank into her neck and I drank her dry.

When I'd satisfied my thirst, I turned, and looked at the crowd that waited behind me.

There was the King. Whose rule we had lived under my entire life. There was my father, Lord Bastian. My mother was a woman who had come and then gone once I was weaned from her breast.

There were other members of the Court. Important people. Some I had known for as long as I could remember. Others who were so close to the king I was seeing them now for the very first time.

"How do you feel, Edith?" my father asked.

I looked at him. At his expectant face, so hopeful. So desperate to be the one to produce the offspring who would finally awaken. "I…" I shook my head. I wanted to take a step back. To retreat into the dark corners of the castle and go back to being one of a dozen human children in Roter Himmel, looked over until their time came. But all eyes were on me. "I don't remember anything."

The King stepped forward. The look in his eyes was dark and complicated. "It takes time, my dear." Slowly, he crossed to me, where the woman laid dead at my feet. The humans still stood lined up, as if waiting to see if the urge for more would strike me. Every one of them waited willingly for me to kill them. "Over the course of the next few weeks, you are a guest at the castle. I'd very much like to get to know you, Lady Edith. And I hope you will not shy away from getting to know me."

He placed a hand at the small of my back, guiding me toward the doorway at the edge of the ballroom.

Scared, so scared and unsure and absolutely over-whelmed, I looked back at my father.

There was a gleam in his eyes, something pleased, and he nodded encouragingly.

I swallowed once, telling myself to be brave, and walked through the doors, to a new place, a new life, side by side with King Cyrus.

A SHIVER WORKS ITS WAY DOWN MY BACK AS I PULL UP TO the curb at The MetroCosmo. A valet immediately comes to my door, opening it for me. I step out, double-checking my sunshades as I climb out.

The sun is just barely beginning to creep into the horizon. I drove all through the night to get here, stopping for gas just once, and draining the attendant of half of his blood.

I think he will survive. I don't think he'll turn to a Bitten.

I hope.

The cars in front of and behind me stop, and guards from the House of Valdez hop out, one man taking my bag from the trunk of my car.

I turn to the incredible doors of the casino, and just then Hector, Raphael, and Edmond walk out.

Where there was once a twinkle of annoyance in his eyes when Hector looked at me, now there is only reverence.

All three of them bow deeply.

"My Queen," each of them mutters.

Logan and Sevan clash. To Sevan, it is so familiar. So

natural. She stands a little straighter, holding her chin high. But Logan wants to recoil and scoff a little.

"Hector," I address him. "Edmond. Raphael. It's a pleasure to meet you...for the first and second time."

They don't know how to react to that, but all three of them do their best to contain it.

"We are honored that you chose to spend time with us in your first hours of Resurrection," Hector says, and I do hear the surprise and humility in his voice. "Though we are surprised to see you here without your husband."

I raise my chin just a little higher and look behind them so I don't have to meet their eyes. "Cyrus had business to attend to back in Roter Himmel, and I had my own."

The growling roar of an engine reverberates against the walls as a huge black truck stops just behind my caravan.

For the first time since I woke up, a little smile curls on my face.

Larkin steps out from the driver's seat. The danger in his eyes is dominant as he walks around to join us at the doors.

He stands over six feet tall, well over two hundred pounds. His dark chocolate skin flows smoothly over heavily muscled arms. His black t-shirt stretches over an even more toned chest. Black boots are strapped about his feet and even though he wears black jeans, I know he's hiding a multitude of weapons on his person.

His eyes remain fixed on my face as he approaches, but he keeps them controlled, hiding his emotions. He stops just three feet from me and takes a deep bow as he takes my hand.

"It is an honor to stand in your presence once more, my Queen," he says in his deep voice.

Briefly, he kisses my knuckles.

"It is good to see you again, Larkin," I say as my smile spreads. He stands, and I don't hesitate in wrapping my arms around his thick middle, resting my cheek against his chest.

I sense it: the entire House of Valdez watching the reunion of their long-dead queen and her most trusted operative. But I don't really care. Right now I'm lost in the overwhelming relief of feeling that for now, just one single thing is right.

"Thank you for coming so quickly," I say as I release him. He only nods once, but I see it there in his eyes now: he's happy to return to me.

"Larkin," Raphael says with a nod. "It's…good to see you again."

His tone says otherwise.

"Come," Hector says, angling his body toward the doors. "Your friend from the House of Conrath is waiting for you."

He stands to the side, waiting for me to enter first. Conflict once more claws its way through my blood as I walk forward. Larkin immediately follows me.

The MetroCosmo is even more impressive as a vampire. My eyes can more fully appreciate the richness of the purples and blues that reflect on the mirrors. My skin tingles with the electric energy.

But my nose feels assaulted.

There's the scent of blood, but most overwhelming are the unwashed bodies after sitting at the tables too long. The stench of cigarettes and alcohol.

I'm beginning to understand a little better why Cyrus dislikes Las Vegas so much.

It's kind of disgusting.

I lead the way to the elevator I've ridden in before. Hector places his hand on the mirror, and the doors open.

"Unless you have another request," he says once everyone is inside and the doors slide closed. "We've placed you in the same room as your last visit."

"That's just fine," I say. And Logan wants to say stop making such a fuss over me and chill.

With impressive speed, we rocket up through the belly of the casino. Up and up and up and then finally we slow, and the doors open. We all step out.

I walk forward and immediately turn left to go to my room when Hector speaks out.

"My Queen," he says. I turn and look back at him, Larkin just to my side. "May I ask: what can we expect from your visit? And how long do you wish to stay?"

And I don't know who it is—Sevan or Logan—who lets the smile curl on my lips. "I'll stay as long as I need. And as for what to expect, just plan to stay on your toes."

I shouldn't appreciate the uncertainty and worry in their eyes so much. But I do. I really do.

I finish the short walk down the hall and place my hand on the mirror. The doors to my suite slide open, and we step inside.

A glittering mirror chandelier hangs from the ceiling in the central lounge room. The lights are dim and low, but still, those purples and reds dazzle me.

But I don't have much attention for them.

Not when my oldest friend from this life sits in a chair, looking at me.

Rath immediately stands, his posture overly at attention, his eyes wide and expectant. "Logan," he breathes. "Are you…are you alright?"

I stop outside the circle of chairs and couches, studying him.

Once more, I search, trying to recall.

But I'm certain.

I've never met Cornelius Rath before this life.

But it's his scent. It's his heart. His blood.

Rath isn't a vampire—Born or Bitten. But he's definitely not human either.

"So it's done then," he says, watching me with regret in his eyes. "You've Resurrected."

I nod once, taking a step closer. Like a shadow, Larkin steps forward as well, and Rath's eyes slide over to him.

"And you know this man?" Rath says, as if sizing him up. Comparing himself to Larkin. And I see the angst in his eyes. The disappointment. Because Eli knows everyone in my life, and Rath does not know this man who stands so protectively near.

"Yes," I confirm. I stop beside a high-backed chair, resting my hand on it. "Larkin is a friend. Someone I trust even more than I once trusted you."

I knew my words would hurt Eli. But he tries to hide it.

And he bows to me, his head sinking low. "Then hail to the Queen." He straightens once more, his expression hardening. "It is an honor to meet you, after hearing of your legend all these years."

I hate that. Every single word he just said. All the formality. The absence of everything familiar between us.

But really, we've been strangers my entire life.

"I have a question," I say. My eyes drop to the chair beside me, but I don't really see anything. "How long were you going to wait? Was there a certain point that you and Alivia agreed that I could finally be told the truth?"

Rath doesn't immediately provide an answer. He hesitates just long enough that I look back up at him.

"Your twenty-fifth birthday," he says. "We were going to wait until then. I was to introduce you to this world, gently. And then Alivia was going to leave it up to you if you wanted to meet her."

Twenty-five. I just turned twenty last month.

I picture it. If it had all gone according to Rath and Alivia's plan, I would have had five more years of normality. Five years of being under Shylock's thumb, in debt. I'd be homeless by this point. I'd be miserable and stubborn, trying to provide for myself when everything was crumbling around me.

I've lost everyone I care about now. Yet I've also opened so many doors to others I had forgotten about.

Like Larkin.

I nod. "Thank you for telling me." I step forward and sink down into the chair, crossing my legs and looking at the man who watched over me nearly my entire human life. "Are you okay?"

It takes him aback, me asking him that question. He blinks twice. "I could use a full two days sleep on a proper bed, but yes, physically I am alright."

I bite my lower lip, considering. "Have you called Alivia Conrath already?"

Slowly, he sinks back into his chair, but never breaks his gaze. "No," he says, shaking his head. "Not that the House of Valdez was going to give me access. But you're a grown woman, Logan. Your interaction with her, and the timing of it, is your decision."

"From what Cyrus has said, you're crazy loyal to her," I say. "I would think you'd be very anxious to share the news."

Rath shakes his head. "In some ways, my relationship with your mother is as complicated as Cyrus'. I have served the House of Conrath for a very long time, and while I will always love Alivia, always wish I had guided her better, I cannot condone so many things she did. I do not know if I will ever be able to forgive her for everything."

Everything he just said startles me. My stomach knots.

"Then why would you spend sixteen years of your life keeping watch over me for her?" I ask, astounded.

Rath crosses one ankle over his knee. "While I love Alivia, my true devotion is to my best friend, the Conrath lost in the dark. It is for your grandfather that I have done what I have done. You are a Conrath by birthright."

My head is spinning. Sevan certainly understands complicated family tress. But Logan can't handle all of this.

Grandfather.

Rath knew my maternal grandfather.

Who is apparently dead.

I shake my head, trying to clear the confusion from my brain.

"What now?" I ask. "Eventually I will return with Cyrus

to Roter Himmel, but not yet. You say meeting my mother is my choice, but what about you? Will you return to the House of Conrath?"

Rath doesn't have words immediately. He studies me, and I know the complex emotions raging through him. They're the same as what is going on inside myself.

"These next few weeks will be tumultuous ones for you, Logan," he says. "I may be loyal to the House of Conrath, and will be until the end of my days, but Logan, sixteen years of hiding a difficult and complicated fate from you doesn't go away because you are upset with me. If you need my help, you have it."

I don't see it coming. But suddenly my throat is tight and emotion bites the back of my eyes. I cross my arms over my chest and have to look away.

I don't know what to say. My pride and bitterness want to send him away, to never see his deceiving face again.

But another part of me knows the value of devotion and loyalty.

I truly don't know what to say.

"We should talk," Larkin says, saving me in the moment of awkwardness.

I stand and head toward my bedroom, grateful. Larkin follows me without a word. I meet Rath's eyes for just a second as I close the bedroom door behind me.

"Are you alright, my queen?" Larkin asks from behind me.

I turn, looking over at him. "Can you…can you please just call me Logan for now?"

He gives a little nod. "Of course, Logan."

I walk to the bed, trailing my fingers over the soft fabric. I feel a little lost, momentarily. "No," I answer the question he posed a few moments ago. "I'm not alright. I feel…" I shake my head. Because I don't know how to answer that question. "I feel like I'm lost in the darkest forest on Immergrun Mountain. Or maybe tossed into Spiegel Lake. I can't tell which way is up, or where home is."

"Do not be too hard on yourself," Larkin says. He watches me from beside the door, his eyes catching every one of my movements. "You've woken up with years of a new life seven times. It is understandable if you need a few days to piece yourself together."

"Eight," I say once more, this time to a different man.

My eyes rise, studying the wall as if it can hold the answers. Find the pieces to that eighth life that I know exists.

"Eight," Larkin says, sounding slightly breathless. "You mean there has been a life between this one as Logan, and La'ei? You returned at some point in the past 286 years?"

I look back at him. My gaze is misty when I nod my head. "I can't remember it yet, but I know it's there. Something…something happened. I just can't remember yet."

He takes one step forward, his eyes fixed on me. "If you wished to discuss the complexities of your life, you would have called someone, perhaps anyone else," he says knowingly. "Not me. Tell me, Logan. Why is it that you had a need to call me?"

I'm relieved. He changes the subject to something I can deal with. Something that may be deadly, but is simple. Something I know how to deal with, because I've been doing it on and off for thousands of years.

"Five days ago, there was an attempt on Cyrus' life," I say, standing straight and facing Larkin. "It was planned, laid out. They weren't particularly smart about it, Cyrus easily killed them. But there was something about it that bothers me."

Larkin's eyes narrow. "What is that?"

"It was a feeble attempt," I say, crossing my arms over my chest. "But the way they did it. It rattled Cyrus. For a day or two before they actually attacked, Cyrus was worried. I got the feeling they'd possibly followed him from Roter Himmel. They knew he was there with no security. Cyrus felt threatened."

"You think it was more about getting into the King's head than the actual attack?" Larkin clarifies.

I nod. "I've rarely seen him shaken. I had to remind him of what he was capable of. Perhaps it was his worry over me, in my human state. But I feel like this was different from other attacks. It's like they knew how Cyrus would react."

I can see the wheels turning in Larkin's head.

There's a reason I called Larkin. This is what he does. This is what he excels at.

"I want you to investigate this," I say. "The attacker was killed. Mina buried his body on the property. But these things are rarely orchestrated by a single individual. I want you to see if there is anything else to worry about."

Larkin's fingers roll into fists and he stands a little taller. "It would be my pleasure," he says. Even his voice sounds deeper.

"It happened in Colorado," I say. "Half a day's drive from here." I turn and find a pad of paper and a pen on the nightstand. I write the address of Cyrus' house in Greendale down and hand it over to him. "Do whatever you have to do to figure out who did this."

He takes the paper, and for just a moment, embers ignite in his eyes. "I'll do whatever it takes to find out who tried to kill your husband, Logan."

I swallow at the title, but nod.

With one last bow, Larkin turns and leaves the room to go hunt down who did this.

I sit on the edge of the bed, staring at the door once he is gone.

In my very, very long existence, there has always been a need for individuals who are skilled in collecting intelligence. For those who can take care of problems silently.

Over the years, Cyrus has had many spies with incredible skill. Ubaldo was his first. Then came Wolfhard. And last I remember there was Raheem, more skilled than any others before him.

I wonder if he's still in Cyrus' service. It's been so long, who knows.

But all this time, at least since my third life, since I lived a life as Helda, Larkin has been the one I could count on. The one with the deadliest hands, the sharpest fangs, and the most silent feet.

There isn't a cell in me that doubts he can solve this mystery.

I stare at the door Larkin walked out of, and suddenly I feel depleted.

This is it. Everything I had planned after telling Cyrus I wouldn't be returning with him to Roter Himmel is finished.

Call Larkin.

Free Rath.

Start the investigation.

Now what?

I flop back on the bed and stare at the ceiling. I'm exhausted just thinking of the possibilities of where I could go from here.

So for right now, I'm just grateful for this bed, and this room, granting me a safe, private place to rest.

CHAPTER 5

My booted feet sent sounds echoing against the stone walls of the castle. With my ladies, we headed from the lower chambers to the kitchen, but the sound of voices, loud, angry, some terrified, stopped me on my route and changed my trajectory.

I turned, walking down the passage and into one of the many great halls.

There, kneeling in the middle of the room, their hands bound behind their backs, were two men. Their clothing was torn, saturated with blood. Their faces, bruised. Cuts marred their skin.

I knew they were human the moment I stepped foot inside.

Before them stood Cyrus. Other guards surrounded him.

"What is going on?" I demanded, my eyes locked on my husband's.

"Wolfhard found who broke into the storehouse a few

days ago," Cyrus said, as he looked back at the humans. "These two were hiding in the tower of the abandoned church. Apparently, they have been watching us for over a week."

I looked back at the men. When they met my gaze, their eyes widened with terror. They physically recoiled from me, as much as they could considering they were bound.

I understood without anyone having to explain.

These two were not part of the human community that lived here in Roter Himmel.

Outside of our safe haven, humans knew nothing of our kind.

"I'm sure they can be reasoned with," I said, as I stepped forward, toward them. "I'm sure they understand the gravity of what this place is. Surely they can keep a secret."

Both of them nodded their heads frantically, a few tears leaking down one of their faces.

But Cyrus' expression hardened. I recognized that familiar set to his lips, his jaw.

"We let them walk and who knows the price they could obtain for information," he said. I felt it growing—the darkness that existed in the man I had loved for so long. It gathered like a physical thing, and all any of us could do was brace ourselves for it.

"Please," one of the men begged. "I only stumbled upon your town while traveling through the pass. I swear on both our lives, we won't breathe a word."

Cyrus' face was stone cold. "I'm afraid I cannot allow that. I value secrecy above all else."

In a blur of a movement, he crossed to them. Gripping

them each by the scalp, he yanked in one clean movement, relieving them of their heads.

Blood sprayed, a warm splash of it flew across my right hand.

Cyrus took a step forward, dropping their heads to the stone floor with a wet thud.

"There are other ways," I said as he walked past me. He paused, listening. "Not everything has to end in death."

I felt him lean in close, and then his lips just lightly brushed over my cheek. "I will do whatever it takes to protect our life, my love. Whatever it takes."

I swallowed as he walked away, my face and hands going numb.

~

SOMEONE BRINGS ME FOOD. I EAT.

Hector sends up a woman for me to feed from, and I drink.

In my past lives I've never gotten control very quickly. But I manage to let go of her before I kill or turn her.

A messenger comes to tell me that if I need anything, all I have to do is ask the House of Valdez and they will do it.

A few hours after dinner, someone drops by a note. It says that Cyrus has arrived in Roter Himmel and it was uneventful. It requests that I send word to let him know I am all right.

Glancing over at my phone on the nightstand, my heart feels pulled in two.

One side is annoyed, angry that Cyrus isn't exactly giving

me the space I asked for. Another is so grateful that he thought to let me know he's safe, and ask if I am, as well.

I remember the look in his eyes just before we parted ways.

And my chest cracks.

I grab my phone.

I'm fine. I'm at the House of Valdez. Thank you for letting me know you're safe.

I send the text to Cyrus.

Instantly, it says it's been read.

A tiny smile forms on my lips.

There's a quiet humming sound suddenly, and the coverings on the window begin retracting, disappearing into the wall. My view of the city slowly opens up.

I walk to it, looking out over the dazzling lights of Las Vegas at night.

I can see everything from up here. Up and down The Strip. There are thousands of people going from place to place. There's an electric excitement that promises a night of sinful possibilities.

I go to the closet and dig through my bag, grateful that the House of Valdez didn't go through my things and hang them up for me. I drag out a dress, bright red and form fitting. Stripping out of my clothes, I change into it. I curl my hair and do dark, smoky makeup. Finally, I strap on some black heels.

Quietly, I open the bedroom door and peek out.

Rath lies on the couch, one arm over his eyes. He snores softly.

Without making a sound, I cross the space to the entry

door. I place my hand on the pad, and silently, it slides open and I slip out.

I'm grateful there's not another soul around as I walk down the hall toward the elevator. I press the button and just five seconds later, the doors slide open and I slip inside.

Alone, I plummet through the casino and the doors open on the ground floor.

If I thought the smell was bad before, it's nothing compared to it now. There are ten times more bodies around, and I realize just how popular The MetroCosmo must be. It's packed. The energy is crazy. The volume is nearly over-whelming. The smell of cigarettes and alcohol nearly knocks me on my ass.

Looking around, searching for familiar faces, and smelling the area for other Born, I work my way through the crowd toward the front doors. I smell someone across the casino, but far enough away to not be spotted.

Without being caught, I slip through the main doors and work my way to the crowded sidewalk. Down a block I quickly walk, making sure to get lost in the crowd and not be spotted.

And finally, I stop. I look around.

I revel in the anonymity.

It won't be long. Cyrus was right. It won't be long until word of my return spreads throughout the world. The House of Valdez might have already told others. It could be slipping down the chain as I stand here.

So I appreciate it, here in this moment that I get to stand here alone. And no one around knows who I am.

No one bows.

No one jumps to fulfill my simplest wishes.

No one looks at me with fear because they know what my husband is capable of.

He isn't your husband, half of me shouts as I set off down the sidewalk. *He's never even told you he loved you. There's no ring on your finger. You've never even kissed the man.*

Not my husband, I think to myself as I cross the street and disappear into the crowd.

I duck into a casino Amelia and I visited when we came here last summer. We weren't even old enough to sit at the tables and play. But we did shop our hearts out. At least as much as our tiny budgets allowed.

I hold my head high and make my way to a table.

I won't claim Cyrus as my husband just yet, but that money is just as much mine as it is his.

Before long there's a good gathering of people at the table. Others begin to gather to watch as the seven of us play. One by one, I take their money, winning three games in a row.

I'm kind of shocked, myself.

I've always had the world's worst luck. I lose money. I don't get lucky winning. So the fact that I'm here, rocking this hand and another, it has nothing to do with me as Logan Pierce, and everything to do with Sevan.

Apparently Sevan is good at gambling.

"I think three is my lucky number," I say as I collect my winnings and turn to leave. The other players and the crowd groan audibly. "Learn this lesson: quit while you're ahead."

I smile as I walk away and go to collect the cash.

I move from one casino to the next, in all stopping three

times to play, in all winning nine games. The money I make is more than I earned in the last year and a half of my life.

Still nothing, in the scale of Sevan's life. But it's major in the scope of being Logan.

The night stretches late, but the energy doesn't fade. The crowds are still thick. The scents of alcohol and drugs and sex grow thicker.

It starts as a little tickle in the back of my throat. I raise my hands to it as I walk down the sidewalk. I swallow once. The heat ignites.

I swallow again. But the temperature rises.

I look around. Thousands of people surround me.

Just one.

I just need one body.

A man walks by himself, stumbling slightly. He looks up, his eyes meeting mine and he looks sheepish, slightly embarrassed at his near fall. But I see the hunger that lights in them. He looks me up and down.

I smile at him. I step to the side, eyeing him as I work my way to a dark alcove.

It's not even hard. I lure him over without a single word.

"And how are you, this very spectacular evening?" he says, cocky and seductive. He steps forward, his hands instantly going to my hips.

One second of the presumptuous pig is all I can take. I smile as I reach forward, lacing my fingers behind his head. I guide him to me, and before he can think this is leading anywhere but to him dropping his pants around his ankles, I sink my fangs into his neck.

I pull. One deep suck.

Another.

Four.

Five draws.

On six, I release him, a satisfied sigh rushing over my lips as I lick his blood from them. As soon as I let him go, he collapses to the ground.

He gives a little groan, rolling his head from one side to the other, as if trying to figure out why his neck hurts.

I wipe at my mouth one last time. I glance back at him over my shoulder before walking away, leaving him in the dark.

He'll be fine. He was drunk enough before he ran into me that he won't remember a thing.

I walk another block, and head into another casino. I just wander this time. No destination in mind. Just traveling among the people.

After ascending a grand flight of stairs, a flashing sign points the way to a club. I follow it, and push open the doors to find loud, thumping music.

Maybe it's the confidence I'm portraying tonight, maybe they can sense just how old my soul really is, but not a person has asked for I.D. all night. I walk right in without anyone even giving a questioning glance my way.

Through the crowd of dancing bodies I make my way. Past intimate couples in booths. Beyond the women and men dressed in little to nothing, serving drinks. At the far side of the club, I find an empty table, and I sit.

Not five seconds later, a woman wearing only a leather bra and a thong comes to take my order.

I may be over two thousand years old in one way, but the

other part of me is only twenty, and honestly, alcohol has never been that appealing.

I order a Coke with lime. Not two minutes later she returns with my drink.

"Either you're one of the few law-abiding underage people in this city, or you're smarter than the rest of us and know alcohol almost never leads to anything good."

I look up and see a man standing at a table just a few feet from me. He's alone. He holds a glass in his hand, though I'd guess he hasn't taken more than a sip from it.

"I'm sure I can't be the only one not drinking in this city," I say, crossing my legs and lifting my chin slightly.

He doubtfully cocks his head just a little to the right. "It's one of the few reasons people flock from all over the world to this city. They can lower their inhibitions and not be judged."

"I don't know," I say, swirling my drink. "I feel a little judged right now."

He laughs and takes a step in my direction, his drink still in hand. His other slips into the pocket of his slacks. "It wasn't my intent. Merely an observation."

He's average height, in good physical shape. His hair is a dirty blonde, maybe needing a cut. Green eyes and a chin that I'm guessing was shaved this morning, from the barely-there hint of five o'clock shadow.

He's overall attractive, in a simple way.

"Are you here by yourself?" I ask, looking around the room. But there are hundreds of people here, he could be attached to any of them.

He stops beside my table and turns, scanning the crowd.

He points to a group of four guys, all dancing and generally looking like fools. "It's my buddy's bachelor party. He's getting married in four days."

"That's exciting," I say, feigning interest.

"Not really," he says, taking a sip of his drink. "She's kind of a nasty person. We're all pretty sure she's marrying him for his money."

I chuckle, shaking my head. "Why aren't you out there looking like an idiot with them?"

He shrugs. "I spent too many years looking like an idiot. Been there, done with that."

He offers a small smile, and something about how normal it is tugs at me.

"Would you like to sit?" I offer. Only because he's being friendly, but not overly flirtatious in a way that makes me instantly recoil.

He smiles again and sinks into the chair beside me.

"I'm Trevor," he says, extending a hand. I shake it.

"Logan," I offer.

"You asked me, so don't think I'm just creeping on you when I ask," he says with a hesitant little chuckle. "But are you here by yourself?"

My eyes go to the crowd. I think about it. About the most familiar people around me in this town, even this state. Who? Edmond? Who I met when he recognized my mother's face and ratted me out to Cyrus? Or Rath—who pretended to be someone he wasn't for my whole life?

"Yes," I answer. Because it's true. And I try to pretend the answer doesn't make my chest hurt.

"I only say this because I'm a junior defense attorney," he

says. "And I've seen a lot of bad, bad things. The Strip really isn't a very good place to go by yourself."

I smile into my glass as I take a sip. "I'm tougher than I look."

He laughs and shakes his head as he takes another drink, finishing it off. He's about to say something when I cut him off.

"Do you want to dance?"

He looks over at me, and I can see it; he's surprised.

I am, too.

He smiles again, stands, and holds a hand out for mine. I take it, and follow him out to the floor.

The music is so loud that it's more noise than actual music. But it pulses, wild and electric. Trevor sets his drink on a table and turns me to face him.

He holds my gaze as he puts one hand on my hip and moves to the music. He's hesitant, going off of my cues. But right now I'm just lonely and so detached from anything real.

I place my hand over his, drawing myself closer.

There's something hypnotic about the environment. The heat in the air. The fact that there's very little room to move around. Our bodies have no choice but to press close together.

He's not your husband, I think to myself.

I turn, my back to his front, letting my eyes slide closed as Trevor's hands once more cling to my hips, pulling them toward his own. I reach up, looping a hand behind his neck.

Louder and louder the music pounds.

It reaches down through my blood. It pours into my heart. It saturates through my pores.

Less and less space exists between our two bodies. I try to eliminate it, one beat at a time, so I don't feel so alone. So I don't feel so lost.

The feel of his lips soft on my shoulder makes my eyes slide closed. Makes my lips part just slightly.

His fingers tighten on my hips and I pray he never lets go.

One hundred bodies moved in perfect synchronization. A stomp. A slide forward. A twirl. A dramatic drop.

My hair brushed the sparkling stone floor, and slowly, he raised me up. My eyes met his as I stood upright. They hide behind his glittering gold mask, but I knew those eyes. Had stared into them for decades and centuries.

He twirled me under his arm once more as the other couples slowly worked to form a circle around us.

But I didn't see them.

I saw the heat in those dark green eyes. And for a moment, I was grateful. That despite our separation, over and over, I had worn four other faces, but his was always the same.

Always my Cyrus.

With my back to his chest, our hands raised together. They crossed in front of my chest, and he pulled me in close.

Gently, his lips touched my shoulder. Slowly slid toward my neck. They rose up, until they were just under my ear.

"I have loved you for centuries, Sevan," Cyrus whispered. "And I swear I will love you for millennia more."

Another pair of lips plays gently just under my ear, and I startle back to the present with a stiff jerk.

I straighten, taking three steps away from Trevor, into the crowd.

I turn, and see the confused, disoriented expression on his face.

"Thank you for the dance, Trevor," I say, grateful that my voice is working better than I expected. "I hope you have some fun with your friends."

He doesn't say anything as I walk away. Just stares after me, his mouth slightly open.

When I break outside of the hotel onto the quieting sidewalk, the breath rips from my chest with a gasp.

I lean against a stone wall down the walk, my hands clutching my chest.

Alone.

Aching.

Both of us.

Both of you are hurting, Logan argues with Sevan. *Damn it. You don't have to do this. We don't have to be alone.*

And my mind wanders back, to just one week ago. When I found Cyrus standing at his bedroom window. Empty. Broken. Alone. I begged him then to tell me what would make him happy. He asked me to stay, and I slept in his arms that night.

For just a few moments, when I woke up the next morning, I was happy.

Staring into his face. I knew what he was capable of. How dangerous he could be. But I also knew how he would do anything to protect me. Staring into his face, I knew I loved that man.

I love Cyrus.

You don't have to hurt this way, Logan whispers to Sevan. *You're hurting yourself. You're hurting him.*

Oh, but you don't remember everything yet, Sevan quietly answers. *We've been through this before. This pain. This recovery. This blending. Over and over. And it's his fault.*

I rub a hand up my arm as my face crumples with emotion. Tears well in my eyes as I stand straight again. My chest is tight and it's hard, so hard to breathe.

Logan's human legs would have shaken on the walk back to the House of Valdez. But Sevan has done this before. Over and over. And she walks back with her chin held high.

CHAPTER 6

THE VERY, VERY FIRST HINTS OF LIGHT DANCE ON THE horizon just as I slip once more through the doors of The MetroCosmo. I recognize a member of the House of Valdez, who stands at the door. The minute I walk past him, he speaks into a device on his wrist, letting someone—everyone —know I have returned to the building.

I head straight to the elevator, place my palm on the glass, and step inside the moment it opens. I rise through the building, and I'm not one bit surprised when the doors open, to see Hector Valdez standing in the main area.

"If you're here to reprimand me for sneaking out, you can save your breath," I say as I step out and walk right past him. "I'm a grown ass woman, I can do what I please."

"Please, my Queen," he says, scrambling to follow me. "It's just that if anything were to happen to you, you know what the King would do to us."

I instantly turn. Grabbing Hector's tie, I spin, backing

him against the wall. His head cracks against it, splintering the mirror.

"I am perfectly capable of taking care of myself," I say, keeping my voice calm and even. "And if you dare breathe a word about any of my comings and goings to Cyrus, you will have more than just him to worry about."

His eyes slip down, to where I hold a broken piece of mirror at the base of his ribcage.

The terror in his eyes is obvious, and I both relish in it and hate it.

I drop the shard and step away, releasing him.

"You won't be bothered by me much longer," I say as I continue walking down the hall to my suite. "I only came here to retrieve Rath. I will be leaving tonight."

I place my hand on the mirror, and the doors slide open. I step inside.

Rath steps out of the bedroom Cyrus once occupied, and I note that he does, indeed, look better rested.

"You have everyone here at the House of Valdez in quite the state of distress," he says.

I note: there's something different about him now, now that I'm Resurrected.

He's so calm and composed. His speech is more formal. There's a deeper darkness in his eyes. Everything about him seems...older.

"They don't need to worry about me," I say as I cross the space. I head to a desk pushed up against one wall and open a drawer to find a piece of paper. "Though I suppose I can sympathize with the pressure they feel from Cyrus."

I find a pen and head to a chair, sinking into the comfortable black leather.

"I am surprised," Rath says, observing me as I begin writing things down. "This…you…everything that has transpired since you Resurrected has not been what I expected."

"How is that?" I ask without looking up.

"The legend of Cyrus' love for Sevan is unprecedented in all of history," he says calmly. "So, the fact that you came here, that Cyrus has returned to Roter Himmel without you, is nothing short of baffling."

"History only tells Cyrus' side of our story." I have to concentrate on not squeezing the pen so hard that it splinters and explodes. "Cyrus does not tell the version where I have to cope with what he did, over and over. It does not tell the story of our fights over right and wrong. He has omitted me begging him to end this, our curse, over and over, through several lifetimes."

I've stopped writing and my eyes stare at nothing, a blank space of floor.

"The story passed down through our descendants captures the beautiful parts of Cyrus and myself. But it is missing all of the darkness."

My chest feels that darkness.

There's a deep, pitch-black cavern inside of me, filled with secrets and lies and tear-filled words.

"I understand," Rath says. "Logan."

I look up at him then, at that name.

For a few moments there, I lost her. She slipped into the shadows of all the others I have been. For just a moment, I was a simple person who just lived one life.

But they all come crashing back now.

I look back down at the notebook in my lap.

"Jafari," I say. My voice is quiet. It holds just a little bit of a tremble. "Helda. Shaku. Antoinette. Edith. Itsuko. La'ei." I close my eyes for a moment, shaking my head. "And Logan. I have been every one of these women. Lived an entire life as them before death. They're all there, but they feel...just out of reach. Out of focus."

Rath slowly crosses the room. He looks over my shoulder at the page.

"Tell me something about Antoinette," he says as he takes a step away and sinks into the chair adjacent to mine.

I look at him, studying his face. The black, curly facial hair that has grown long on his face over the last month. His hair is long, too, far longer than I've ever seen it.

But those are the same familiar lips, set in a serious line. Those same eyes that have seen far more than I ever realized.

"Antoinette was born at Court," I say, and instantly I can see it. The beautiful landscape of Roter Himmel. The hustle of bodies, Royal and human, living side by side. The gowns and the food. The midnight parades through the streets. "Our father, Lord Gadox had only one wife. They'd been lucky, they were able to conceive three children, three years in a row."

I smile as I recall their faces. "I had one older sister and one younger. And we were a happy family. My parents loved one another. They loved us children. They took us on weekly boat rides on Spiegel Lake. Trips into the mountains. My mother baked the most wonderful bread every morning."

My brows furrow and fall to the page, focusing on the name I bore for nineteen years.

"A Royal with three Royal daughters drew a lot of attention in Roter Himmel," I remember. "During that time, there was only one other female Royal born. You know how close Cyrus has kept an eye on the female descendants." My eyes lose their focus, recalling the moments of tension leading up to the knock on the door that came once every six months. "Cyrus came to see us very often. Twice a year, from the time we were born, he would visit our home. He was always so happy. His eyes held so much excitement."

My skin crawls, remembering what that meant to me when I was old enough to understand why he came to see me and my sisters.

"Cyrus favored my older sister," I continue. "Aimée. He never said it, but I could see it in his eyes, he thought she would be the one when we Resurrected. He paid her the most attention. And I was grateful for it. If she was the Queen, I didn't need to worry about it. I could simply plan my life, decide what my fate would be once I was immortal."

Emotion bites at the back of my eyes and I shake my head. It comes back, clearer and faster, the more I talk about it. "We were sisters, had been so close our entire lives. We were close in age, so Cyrus allowed us to wait to Resurrect all at the same time."

Goose bumps rise on my skin as I remember walking to the castle with my family. It was a great procession. Everyone in the entire town came to watch the Gadox sisters go to end their lives as human and wait to see if they were the one, Cyrus' long lost wife, who had been dead for seventy-six years.

"We did it in one of the grand ballrooms at the castle," I resume the story of Antoinette. "We stood in a row, Cyrus seated on his throne before us, Sevan's empty one beside him. Three guards stood behind us, and drove a dagger through our hearts."

A gasp slips over my lips now, and my hand rises to my chest, remembering those two seconds of agonizing, blinding pain. The feel of warmth slipping down my chest.

And then the dark.

"I woke four days later, at the exact same moment as my sisters," I say. "For two weeks, we were pampered guests at the castle, spending nearly every moment with Cyrus. Cyrus watched Aimée so closely. Spent so much time flattering her and making her laugh.

"But then as I walked passed a door, I had a...vision," I say. "A memory. I knew there was a passageway to the treasury behind that door. I spent the rest of that day wandering the castle, and one by one, I knew where every single door led. Slowly, I could recall cleaning the debris from the castle. I remembered Cyrus spending hours fixing it. And I remembered the way our son's infant cries reverberated throughout the entire castle the first night we slept in it."

My throat closes up and I can't speak as I recall an angelic face.

But like a door being slammed closed, my memory goes dark, blocking it out.

"It took me another month to forgive Cyrus for the attention he gave my sister," I say. "It was petty, and I knew he was only relying on hope and instinct. But it was still difficult, thinking he didn't recognize me, even though I'd been there in front of him for so long."

"It's understandable," Rath says, and I actually flinch. I had forgotten he was here. "Sevan, I cannot even imagine how difficult this must be for you."

I look up at his face, and I'm filled with wonder.

Rath is very good at reading people. He's good at reading the multiple people inside of me.

He knows when to address Logan, and he knows when to address Sevan.

I nod, settling back further into my chair, suddenly feeling exhausted. I'm trying to pull all these lives together, back to the surface, and consolidate them into one.

I look back down at the paper. "I don't remember everything. And I'm not a very patient person. I might as well use the resources at hand, right?"

I stand and with my paper and pen, I head toward the door. But I stop just in front of it. I look back at Rath.

"You're free to go wherever you like," I say. Stupid Rath. He's just one more man that makes my heart feel all tangled into complicated knots that can never be untied. "I'll make sure no one from Court or the House of Valdez bothers you. You can return to Alivia if you like, or go wherever."

He stands, staring at me, history and knowledge in his eyes. "I've served in some capacity or another my entire life. Right now, I see a woman who needs someone on her side, no matter who she is. I told you that I'm here for you."

Rath may not be Eli, like I'd always thought. But he's still here, supporting and protecting me.

I smile.

"Come on, then," I say as I nod toward the door.

Together, we walk down the hall, to the elevator. We rise up a floor, and the doors open.

"Please find Hector, Edmond, and Rafael and tell them that I need to speak with them. Now," I say to a House member who looks at me with questioning eyes as I head straight into the ballroom. But he scrambles and heads off to search.

I'm feeling bold. And even though Logan thinks this is weird and crazy, I head straight for Cyrus' throne, which still sits at the head of the room.

My heart rate picks up a bit as I lower myself into it.

Rath slips in beside me, standing silent and solid, waiting.

I have to wait for five minutes. And then Edmond and Hector come out of the elevator. As they cross the ballroom, once again it opens, and out steps Rafael.

"My Queen," Hector says as they all step in front of me. He takes a deep bow, which is immediately mimicked by his two sons.

"I'm hoping that you might be able to help me," I say as they stand up. "I know you all are wondering why I came here without Cyrus. I don't feel obligated to give you any kind of an explanation, but I will say this: when I return to Roter Himmel, and the entire world knows I've Resurrected once more, I need to have my shit together, and right now I have the memories of nine people racing around in my head."

The look in their eyes changes from worried anticipation to confusion.

"I was dead for a damn long time," I say, leaning forward

slightly. Logan's spitfire words are taking the lead at the moment. "My timeframe of who I was and when is a little out of focus. So I'm really hoping that the three of you will be able to help me sort a few details out."

"Of course, anything, my Queen," Hector says.

I can practically taste his anxiety and fear.

It may be their King they truly fear, but Sevan certainly isn't someone to be taken lightly.

I hold out the paper with the names written down. "I remember names," I say. "All the women I was. Am. What I don't remember is who I was when, or where, for most of them. I'm hoping some of you are old enough to have heard of some of my past lives."

Rafael looks nervously at his father, who gives him a look in return.

"None of you are particularly old, are you?" I say in annoyance.

"I'm sorry, my Queen," Edmond says, stepping forward. "My father only inherited the House about ninety years ago when his father was killed. Rafael is the oldest, and he's only been Resurrected for fifty-one years."

"I don't feel young," Hector says, stepping forward, his eyes falling to the floor. "But my one hundred and twenty-two years is nothing compared to your timeline, Sevan."

I let out a slow breath through my nose, my fingers curling around the end of the armrest. "Just look at the list, and tell me if anything jumps out at you."

Hector takes it from my hands, and his sons gather around to study the names I have written down. Quietly they read them, and I can feel their stress rolling off them in palpable waves.

Sevan doesn't really care.

"I remember hearing that the last time you were found, it was at the House in Borneo," Rafael speaks up. "It's the House that rules over all those islands, the Pacific. La'ei sounds like a name from the islands."

An image flashes through my head. That of a beautiful cottage by the sea. A white, sandy beach led straight down to crystal clear blue water.

"I would guess that you were her last," Rafael says.

Larkin said this, I remember now, and can put it into perspective.

My gaze is out of focus, but I nod. I'm searching, tracing steps back through that cottage, searching for anything else, grasping for details about my life as La'ei.

A reflection comes to mind, caught in an old mirror. Of long, thick, curly hair. Darker skin and big brown eyes.

I shake my head. "Good," I say. "What about any of the others?"

They all look at the list again. "I can only make guesses based on the origins of the names," Edmond says. "Helda sounds Eurpoean, maybe Germany? Shaku, perhaps Middle Eastern."

"Jafari," Hector says. "I would say that is African."

As soon as he says the words, I feel heat wash across my skin. My eyes squint closed against the sand that blows in them. And sand is all I can see. It spreads out before me for miles on end.

"Is there anything else?" I ask. "Anything that rings a bell?"

The three of them look down at the list again, contemplating for a moment.

"I'm sorry, my Queen," Hector says. "That is all we can speculate."

Speculate. What an infuriating word.

I have nearly no more answers than when I walked in here.

"Thank you," I still say, fighting to control my tone. "If you'll send someone to my room after dinner to collect my bag, Rath and I plan to leave as soon as it's dark."

"Yes, your Maj-"

But he's cut off as the elevator doors to the ballroom slide open and a great roar of anger fills the space.

Every ounce of blood in my body drops out through the bottom of my feet, and instantly I am just one person again.

Brilliantly glowing yellow eyes wildly search the room, in such stark contrast to the dark skin. Despite his thin frame, he bucks and jerks from the grasp of the two Born who haul him into the center of the ballroom.

"Eshan!" I yell, darting up from the throne and rushing over to him. I reach out, but the guards drag him back away from me two steps.

"You let him go right now, you piece of shit!" I bellow, taking another step forward as they once more drag him back from me. "That is my brother!"

"You really don't want us letting him go," one of the guards says. "He's out of control!"

And it's true. Despite him looking directly at me multiple times, he doesn't seem to recognize me.

All his attention is directly focused on Rath.

Eshan jerks against the guards hold, an animalistic roar ripping from his chest. He tries to lunge, over and over.

I see it then. The smear of blood on his chin. The splashes of it on his chest.

"Why is your human brother showing up on the steps of the House of Valdez as a Bitten?" Hector demands. He takes seven steps toward us, his eyes igniting blood red. "Are you trying to get me and my entire House exterminated by your husband?"

"Excuse me?" I hiss, rounding on him. "I left Colorado two days ago with my brother safe and sound, and human. Who the hell brought him here and turned him?"

As if the energy is running out of him, Eshan stops fighting. His eyes seem more able to focus, and suddenly they dart to me.

"Logan?" he says, a scared quake to his voice. "What the hell is going on? Why...why are you here with these people? You said you were going to Austria with Collin."

"Eshan," I say, taking a step toward him. He recoils from me slightly. "E, did you follow me here?"

His eyes dart around, still glowing yellow, but filled with fear. "I knew something wasn't right. I knew you were lying. I don't know, something about Collin and you, it didn't seem right. I followed to make sure you were okay."

My heart cracks. My little brother, four years younger than myself, looking out for me because he thought the man I told everyone was my boyfriend was going to do something to me.

I round on Hector. "It wasn't me who turned him, so you've obviously got someone with a control problem in your House."

Hector looks up at the guards. "Explain."

One speaks up. "I caught him sneaking into the casino. There was blood on his face, his eyes were all lit up. He was looking for a meal. We brought him here so you could dispose of him yourself."

"Like hell you will!" I yell, turning back to Hector. "You're going to find whoever did this to my little brother and deal with *them*, according to the new law!"

"According to the new law, they *will* be dealt with," Hector says, his voice rising. "But according to the new law, *his existence* is also forbidden."

Edmond reaches into his pocket and produces a stake. With determination, he stalks forward, his eyes trained on my brother.

With a demonic roar, I dart across the ballroom in a blur, my fingers snapping around his throat. I shove, throwing him back, and he flies across the ballroom. With a hiss, I turn, baring my fangs at Rafael as he approaches with yet another stake.

"This woman is your queen!" Rath suddenly bellows. Power fills his voice, taking up every inch of this space. "She and her husband made your laws. She has the power to counter those Cyrus put into effect. If you value your life and position, I suggest you let your queen deal with this issue on her own."

They all stand frozen. Looks of annoyance that Rath… whatever he is…has commanded them as if he's allowed to do it, fill their faces. But they also look over at me, and as I stand straight, my eyes glowing brilliant and bright, they all back off a step. Bowing to their Queen.

"Logan," Eshan says. And his breathing grows hard again. I look to see him beginning to tug against the guards once more. "What is happening to me?"

I hear a faint whistling sound and Eshan makes a sound of pain. I see a tiny dart sticking out of the side of his neck.

He roars in pain, all the tendons in his neck straining against his skin. And suddenly he collapses, limp.

With wide, shocked eyes, I turn.

Rath lowers something, sliding it into his pocket.

A blow dart.

"He will be fine," he explains. "He will only sleep for twelve hours. When he wakes we can be prepared."

I shake my head at the whiplash change, but turn, standing straight. I look back at Hector.

"I'm taking my brother with me," I say clearly. "Like I said, we need something to eat first. But as soon as it gets dark, the three of us are leaving. Tell your people to have my things ready by then."

Without waiting for their response, I walk forward. I take my brother from the guards, who don't seem to know what to do. Like he weighs nothing at all, I lift my nearly six foot tall brother up and sling him across my shoulders.

Together, Rath and I go to the elevator. We descend two floors and deposit Eshan onto my bed.

He lies there, looking peaceful, his eyes closed.

"He's really okay?" I ask. Because honestly, he could be dead.

"He's fine," Rath says. "It's a serum that's been tested hundreds, if not thousands, of times."

I shake my head, looking at my brother. "How the hell did this happen?"

"He followed you," Rath says, trying to piece it together for me. "I can only assume while watching you, a local Born grabbed him. When the individual realized their lack of control, they must have fled, leaving your poor brother to wake, not knowing what had happened to him."

I shake my head. "What am I supposed to do?" I say. "My parents will be devastated. I'm going to have to stay with him for the rest of his life, because everyone in the world now knows the Bitten are a death sentence."

"It doesn't have to stay that way," Rath says. The volume of his voice drops and he looks around, as if to make sure no one can hear him.

My brows furrow. "What is that supposed to mean?"

"It means, this does not have to be your brother's fate for the rest of his life," Rath says. "There's a cure. He can be human again."

My eyes grow wide, and I blink. Twice. Three times. Four.

"There is a cure, and somehow, even you, know about it?"

Rath looks around again. "Even Cyrus knows about it. Though he's forbidden its further use."

I blink again, shaking my head.

"There's a lot of history here, Sevan," Rath says. "You

may not want all the answers to your current questions. It's safer for a lot of people you may someday come to care about if you don't know everything. But there is a cure, and I'm sure it's what you want for your brother right now."

"Yes!" I say, getting annoyed. "Yes, it's what I want. Obviously!"

Rath lets out a slow little breath through his nose and looks away from me. "I hope you want it bad enough to go where you must to obtain it."

My blood chills as I think of the possibilities. But I know, I'd go anywhere to get my brother this cure. "Where?"

Rath looks back and meets my eyes, and I see it in his own: he's not exactly thrilled about it either. "The House of Conrath."

CHAPTER 7

It's a twenty-two hour drive from The Strip to Silent Bend, Mississippi.

It's a long-ass drive. But not near freaking long enough.

The moment it is dark outside, Rath and I load Eshan into the backseat of Cyrus' convertible. The House of Valdez packs our bags in the trunk, and say good riddance.

I take Eshan's phone and text our parents, pretending to be him. I make up some story about going to meet some girl he met online. I apologize for worrying them, but promise I'm safe and that I'll be back in a few days.

I didn't know if it's true. But it's something.

After the message sends, I shut his phone off completely so they can't call or track him.

What a freaking mess.

We take off into the night, with nine hours until Eshan will wake up.

I grip the steering wheel as we drive, rocketing through the night on a cross-country trip.

We could have flown. We could have chartered a private jet and arrived in Mississippi before Eshan even woke up and could cause a problem.

But I'm about to meet my birth mother for the first time. I'm about to look the woman who toyed with Cyrus' heart in the eye for the first time. I'm about to face this family Cyrus has told me so much and so little about.

And I'm not freaking ready.

I would have delayed this day for weeks. Months. Maybe even years.

But for Eshan, for my baby brother, I'll face one of my greatest fears.

"I think you should call her," I say as we cross the border of Arizona into New Mexico. "I wouldn't want this sprung on me. She deserves to have a little bit of time to prepare."

I look over at Rath. He's always so serious. Right now is no different.

He pulls out his cell phone and clicks on a name. He holds it up to his ear, and waits as it rings.

"Rath?" a female voice answers. She sounds panicked. "Holy hell, it's been forever since you checked in. I almost sent Anna to come looking for you. Is everything alright?"

"It is, Alivia," he says, and his eyes slide over to mine.

Goosebumps wash over my skin.

That's her. I can hear her voice.

My birth mother.

"Things have indeed happened over the past month," Rath continues. "Nothing went as planned. I…" he hesitates.

"I failed you, Alivia. And your worst fear, indeed, came to pass."

"She is…" I hear Alivia trail off. I even hear her swallow once. "I always knew, but… Was it Cyrus? Did he find her?"

My heart cracks. Because the fear and concern I hear in Alivia Ryan Conrath's voice is so genuine. I think back on all the things Cyrus has said about her, all the bad things I've heard. But what she says…

It's how I imagine my mom sounding.

"Yes," Rath confirms for Alivia. "But he has returned to Roter Himmel."

I hear a soft cry come through on the phone. She doesn't say anything.

"Alivia, Logan is with me," Rath moves on. "Her adopted brother was turned. He needs the cure. We're on our way to Silent Bend now."

Silence. We're met with absolute silence.

The sound of a breath. Quietly, as if from farther away, I hear a male voice. "Alivia?" it asks with concern.

"How soon will you get here?" she finally finds her voice.

Rath looks out at the dark road ahead of us. "We're driving. We were in Las Vegas, at the House of Valdez. We will drive straight through the nights. So it should be two nights from now."

Another long moment of silence. And then a little huff of a laugh. "After all this time. I'm going to meet her in two days?"

I feel it more than see it. The little smile that forms on Rath's lips. "After all this time."

Another breathy laugh comes through the phone. "How... how much of the family do you think she wants to meet?"

Rath looks over at me, and I'm pretty sure all of my internal organs disappear. I keep my eyes fixed on the road ahead of us.

I consider that for a moment. How much of the family? What does that mean? She's my mother. That's all there is.

But that's not true. Cyrus has talked about my cousin. And her mother. And there's my mother's husband.

It's something you should know about the House of Conrath. We're a family here in the House of Valdez. But not like they are. They're family. *The loyalty in that House? I've never seen anything quite like it. They've died for each other. They'd do it again. All of them.*

I take a deep breath. I lift my chin just a little. "Might as well get it all over with in one go," I say quietly.

Rath does another one of those smiles that is barely even there. "All of them," he responds to Alivia.

CHAPTER 8

WE ROLL INTO ALBUQUERQUE JUST BEFORE THE SUN BEGINS to rise. Rath checks into a hotel, getting two rooms. When he returns with keys, we park around back and I carry Eshan into one of the two.

"I can stay," Rath says as he hesitates in the door, looking down at my brother on one of the two beds.

I shake my head. "You smell too human," I say. "Things might be…different between us, but I won't risk him hurting you. Let me deal with him until dark."

Rath meets my eyes, and I can see he wants to argue. But he just nods.

He reaches into his pocket and removes another one of those darts. "If he gets too difficult to handle, you can use another one of these. I have just one more. It won't cover our entire journey back, but it will help."

I take it, careful not to prick myself. "Thank you. I can manage."

He gives a little nod, and walks out the door, to the next room over.

Almost as if on cue, the moment I close and lock the door, Eshan's right foot twitches.

I cross to the insulated bag lying next to the door. The House of Valdez gave me a cooler with six bags of donated blood before we left. I pull one out now.

I sit on the edge of the bed, looking down at my brother. His eyelids twitch once. His hand curls into a little fist.

And with a gasp, he sits up, his yellow eyes flying open. His fangs lengthen, and he goes to leap out of the bed.

I slam my hand against his chest, pushing him back down. I shove the blood bag toward him. One sniff, and he can smell what it is. His instincts take over, and he bites into it. He sucks hard, his eyes sliding closed and a little moan draws over his lips.

A streak of blood slips down his chin.

I watch him as he drinks. I try not to feel sick. I try to keep the horror from my face. I try to remember that I've dealt with this before, on dozens of occasions.

But all I can see is my baby brother drinking human blood.

When he's sucked it dry, he flops back on the bed, dropping the blood bag. His motions are very slow. He wipes at the blood on his chin, looking at it smeared on his fingers.

His hand shakes.

"Eshan," I say quietly.

As if he forgot or didn't realize I was here, he startles, his eyes jerking to me. He scrambles back, curling in on himself against the headboard.

"Lo...Logan?" he says, eyeing me with fear. "What's going on? What happened to me? To you?"

I feel my face blanch. "Me?"

His eyes narrow. "Don't play dumb with me, Logan," he says accusingly. "I followed you the other night. I watched you...bite that guy. Drink his blood. And then just after you went back into the casino, some woman grabbed me and bit me! What..." he struggles to find the words. "What the hell is happening all of a sudden? The world is getting taken over by vampires?"

Vampires. Without a word of explanation, he jumps to the right conclusion.

How couldn't he? He knows what he just drank, what he's still craving now. He's seen what he's seen.

"It could be taken over, but we've been keeping them under control for a long time," I say, looking away from him. "This, what we are now, it's been going on in the shadows for thousands of years. We just didn't know about it before."

I look back up at my brother. His face is contorting with anger. Confusion. Rage. "This has everything to do with Collin, doesn't it?" he says, his voice accusing. "I knew something wasn't right with him. He was just too...too... He did this to you, didn't he?"

My mouth opens, but I'm not sure how to answer that. "No," I say. "Yes. It's...Eshan, this is huge. There's so much to it and I'm still figuring it all out myself. And what about you? What the hell were you thinking? Following me? Do you have any idea how mad Mom and Dad are?"

Sheepishly, he looks at me. "I was worried about you. I knew something wasn't right."

I let out a slow breath, shaking my head.

Dumb, sweet little brother.

"Well, don't turn your phone back on for a while," I say. "We can't have them tracking us until we figure some things out."

Slowly, Eshan relaxes. He looks toward the window. He takes in a deep breath, smelling the air. "What about Eli? I know it's crazy, but I can smell him. He doesn't smell like you, or me, but he doesn't smell like all those people in the casino, either. Is he like us?"

I shake my head and shrug. "I'm not really sure what he is," I say honestly.

His eyes slide back over to mine. "Well, can you please explain what you *do* know?"

CHAPTER 9

"You've never even slept with anyone, but technically you're already married," Eshan says from the back seat.

He's been talking nonstop since we got back in the car.

I explained everything I knew throughout the day yesterday. He drank bag after bag of blood to sate his thirst, even though he said it tasted like it had dirt mixed into it compared to the fresh stuff.

And then once we got into the car to continue driving, Eshan peppered Rath with question after question about his real identity.

He sips on a bag of blood in the back seat. I can feel his eyes on the back of my head.

Rath got more blood from somewhere. I wasn't going to ask where. But Eshan isn't trying to kill Rath so long as he keeps sucking down the donor blood.

"Technically, I don't know how to answer that question,"

I say, tightening my grip on the steering wheel. "Sevan and Cyrus got married a really, really, really long time ago. I never walked down the aisle with this face. Hell, I've never even kissed the man with these lips."

"That is more than enough detail," he says, barely reigning in a gag. "You might be this…Sevan, and Antoinette, and Edith, and La'ei, but you're also still my sister. My sister who pooped her pants once in the fifth grade and tried to say she sat in chocolate."

"I was sick, you little asshole!" I yell, glaring at him in the rearview mirror. "I didn't mean for…that, to happen! Why'd you have to go and bring that up!"

Rath chuckles in the passenger seat, but turns his face and looks out the window.

"Because all of a sudden I find out my sister is the Queen of all vampires!" Eshan continues, relishing in this. "I had to take you down a few pegs! It's my duty as a little brother to keep you humble!"

"Jerk," I say. But a smile is pulling at my lips as I shake my head.

We drive through the night. Texas is huge. So huge. It takes forever and ever to cross, and we only make it to Dallas before the sun starts showing signs of rising, and Eshan starts freaking out about how his eyes are burning already.

We pull off the freeway and head to the first hotel we can find. I check in, getting two rooms once more.

"I think the two of you could use a little bonding time," I say as I haul my bag to one of the rooms. I open it, stepping half inside. "And I need a little break from the forced humility."

With a tight little-lipped smile at my brother, and a quick glance at Eli, I hope that if Eshan loses control, Rath will be quick enough to knock him out with one of the darts.

Some quiet at last, I sigh as I close the door behind me.

I drop my bag on the bed and head straight for the shower. Turning it on burning hot, I step in and start scrubbing myself clean.

It's incredible, such a simple thing. Running water inside a building. Water that is instantly heated. Water that cascades from above and then runs out a drain in the ground.

I think back, once more trying to piece together a timeframe. I can't recall ever having running water in any of my past lives. As Logan, I try to think back through history class, to remember how long running water has been a thing in homes.

Maybe the 1800's?

So it's been since before then that I last died.

Cyrus said it's been 286 years.

Once more that hint of a forgotten life, the seventh life I've lived, the eight death, floats in the recesses of my mind.

But I just can't quite grasp it.

When I finish washing my hair, I step out of the shower, wrapping a towel around my body. I brush my hair and then braid it. Digging through my bag, I pull on some underwear and a tank top.

I can sense it out there, the sun. I stand behind the blackout curtains, imagining the sunrise outside. Imagining how it could warm my skin.

My relationship with it will never be the same. Yes, I've seen Cyrus go out in the middle of the day with the aid of sunshades. Yes, I've used them. But from now on—for the rest of my life, I'll have to think about it before I just go outside.

But in the same breath, this is just natural. I've lived hundreds of years in the dark. Night is natural. Day is the enemy.

So, with that reminder, I turn and climb into the bed. My eyes feel heavy. My brain a little sluggish. It's been five days since I Resurrected, and I haven't slept at all since then.

I slip under the covers, close my eyes, and finally sleep.

I STOOD IN THE HALL LEADING TO THE GRAND BALLROOM. I wore one of the most elegant gowns I'd ever seen. The fabric was a deep, royal purple. Golden stitching made intricate patterns all over the surface. The back of it laced up, cinching me in tight. And atop my head sat my crown. Simple and gold. The one I'd worn for so long.

I could hear them all inside the ballroom. The orchestra playing a complicated melody. The hundreds of bodies dancing. Voices speaking of politics and families and love.

I stood out in the hall by myself. Just staring at the great wooden doors.

It was a party. The House in France recently passed leadership to a daughter. She was loved. Respected. Those from the area were exceedingly glad to be rid of her father and have her take his place.

Cyrus had invited them here, to Roter Himmel as his guests. He wanted to get to know this woman. He wanted to understand her so he would know how to control her if the need arose.

In truth, it really was just another party.

But I stood there, staring at the great wooden doors.

I was dressed for the part. I was ready to step into that ballroom, have all those eyes fall on me. Hundreds would bow to me in respect.

But I just…

I couldn't. Not today.

I turned, ready to go back to my rooms. But the doors swung open, just enough to allow one person to slide through.

I met Cyrus' eyes, and everything in me stilled.

His eyes were the first part of him that I fell in love with. So penetrating, like he could read my very soul like it was a book. I loved their intensity, even if it sometimes frightened me just a little.

He used that look as he slowly walked toward me.

I took in a breath as he reached me. Time. Mountains. Sandalwood.

I even loved the way Cyrus smelled.

"What is it, my love?" he asked as he took my hands in his. He pressed my palms flat to his chest, holding his hands over mine. "What is the matter?"

I looked away from him, over his shoulder, to those huge wooden doors. "I just can't today, *im yndmisht srtov*," I said as I shook my head. "All the games. The posturing. The politics. I just can't today."

Emotion pricked my eyes and my chest felt tight.

So long. We'd been alive for so long. Done all of this for

such a long time.

"Do you ever get tired of it?" I breathed. "Do you ever wish it would all just disappear?"

My eyes slid back to his. He didn't answer right away. He gazed at me, and I could see him thinking, considering all I just asked.

And I understood. Because when I thought about it, all that Cyrus had accomplished, it's incredible. There isn't a word big enough for it.

"When I look at you in the mornings, standing at the window, looking over the land, with the weight of the world on your shoulders, weighing you down, I wish it would all disappear," he said. His voice was low, intimate. The words just between the two of us. "When I see you sitting on your throne, alone in a room full of subjects, a look of distance in your eyes, I wish it would all disappear." He drew me closer. He touched his forehead to mine, and we breathed the same air. The heat of his body warmed me. "When we lie in bed, and someone walks in with complications that must be dealt with, and I see the disappointment in your eyes, I wish it would all disappear."

My eyes slid closed as his words wrapped around me in a warm, soft embrace. I leaned into him, resting my forehead in the crook of his shoulder and neck. He took my right hand in his left, cradling it gently against his chest. His other wrapped around my waist.

Slowly, he began swaying us to the music. Gentle, tiny movements. I clung to him, relishing in his strength and solid presence. I breathed in his air, letting it fill me.

Together.

As one.

We swayed gently back and forth.

He softly hummed. They weren't the exact notes that the orchestra played in the ballroom, but they matched the melody. It was a love song. One about all the pain we'd endured together. But also all the nights in each other's arms. The kisses shared in passageways. The acts of kindness and patience. The shared tears over grief that would never go away, no matter how long we lived, over a child lost long before his death.

Softly, Cyrus hummed the song of us.

"I want to go somewhere," I said quietly against my husband's skin. "Just you and I. For a long while. Just as husband and wife."

I looked up, to stare into his beautiful face. And I loved all the devotion I saw in his eyes, and I felt it in myself; this man had made some bad choices. Made lifetimes of mistakes. But I would do anything for him. I would never, ever love another as I loved him.

"Anything, *im yndmisht srtov*," he promised. And slowly, he leaned forward, and took my lips as his. Forever.

MY HANDS IMMEDIATELY CLING TO MY CHEST. THE HOLLOW ache in it makes it nearly impossible to breathe. Tears immediately spring into my eyes. I can't stop them. They silently cascade down my face, saturating my pillow.

I sob. I reach across the bed, searching for a warm body, or even just a warm space beside me, but the sheets are cool and empty.

A bone-rattling breath sucks into my chest and I curl into a ball on my side.

Cyrus may have created his own curse that he shared with so many others, but this is my own: to love a man who did such a horrible thing to me. To ache for him in the same breath that I hate him. To crave his touch and nearness, even as I have to piece the puzzle of my identity together, over and over.

But no matter what, I always end up at the same place. I want him with me.

Even if right now, it's the last thing I need.

Rolling over, I search for my phone on the nightstand. The screen blinds me momentarily when I wake it. I don't even have any choice in it when my fingers scroll through the names and click the one.

It rings only twice before it connects.

"*Im yndmisht srtov*," Cyrus breathes over the line.

"Cyrus," I whisper. And the moment his name crosses my lips, emotion splits my chest. More tears force their way down my face. I cover my mouth with my hand to hold in the sob that wants to rip from me.

"What's wrong?" he breathes. "Tell me where you are and I will be right there." And I do hear him moving. I hear others in the background, jumping to fulfill his needs, speaking in German.

"No," I whisper. "I'm fine. You don't..." But I don't know what to tell him. I don't know how to vocalize what is going on inside of me. "Can you just... Can you just lie here with me?"

He's quiet for a long moment. The only thing I hear is the

sound of his breathing, but just barely.

And then he pulls the phone away from him as he sends those around him away. Once more I hear him walking. And I just listen to him. I absorb the familiar sounds of his breathing.

Through this little electronic device, I can feel him. Can nearly touch his presence. Cyrus is that strong. That commanding. That tangible.

The soft sound of a door clicking shut comes through, and then rustling.

I can picture it. Him crossing our room. The enormous canopy bed. Him climbing into it.

"I'm here, my love," he finally says to me.

His voice.

Oh, his voice.

I clutch the fabric at my chest, as if I can hold my own heart and keep it from splintering into a million little shards.

My throat is tight.

"Talk to me, *im yndmisht srtov*," he requests. His voice is nervous. Hesitant.

"I don't know if I have anything to say," I whisper. "I just... I needed to hear your voice."

"I cannot express how grateful I am to hear yours," he says. "The past four days have felt like four years."

The words *I'm sorry* are right there at the end of my tongue, but I hold them in. Because I am, but I'm not. "They have been long for me, too."

There's another long pause, as both of us search for words to express this moment.

"I've told no one here at Court," he says. "Mina and

Fredrick have sworn silence. The time and manner is yours, whenever you choose."

I nod, even though he can't see it. Tears of gratitude cascade down my face. "Thank you," I say quietly.

Once more, we're both quiet.

But right now I'm imagining him lying there in the bed. One of his arms is hooked behind his head. He stares up at the black crystal chandelier that hangs high above it. The stones of the ceiling are familiar. But he's not really seeing any of that. He's seeing us, slowly dancing alone out in the hall. Alone, just the two of us.

"We never took that trip," I say. My voice is little more than a whisper. "With just you and I. Together. Just husband and wife again."

I hear just the smallest of breaths catch in his throat. I know what my remembering the little details of our past together means to him.

I know what it means to me.

"Do you remember what we planned?" he asks gently.

More tears push out of my eyes as I squeeze them closed. I shake my head. "No," I admit. "Will you tell me?"

"That very night we began to plan it," he tells our story, reminding me. "We were to depart in three weeks. You had always heard incredible things about India. We were going to go to the jungle and then the beach. No timeframe. Just however long we needed, just you and I."

His words thicken. And he stops speaking for a long while.

Cyrus is a harsh and cold man to everyone who knows him, even to those who don't.

But I know the emotion he's capable of.

He fights to gain control over it now.

"Why did we never go?" I ask when he does not continue. Through the ransacked cavern of my memories, I search. I try to find the reason. Surely it must be there, somewhere.

"Because you got sick just four days after we planned it," Cyrus says. His words come out sharp and filled with emotion. "Four days later, you drained not one, but two of the feeders. Five days later you felt too tired to get out of bed. Seven days later, you went through a dozen feeders, and it was never enough."

His voice cracks and he suddenly goes quiet.

More tears roll down my face, but not for myself.

I can picture his face. How it is crumpled in emotion. How his skin grows red. How his lips quiver. How he holds a hand over his eyes, trying to rub out the emotions.

A small sob slips between my lips. Once more I cover my mouth with my hand, trying to hold myself together.

"Twelve days after we planned that trip, I held you in my arms as you looked up at me. You were too weak to move. But tears trailed down your cheeks as you looked up at me." Cyrus' voice trembles as he tells me the story.

And I realize, I don't remember any of them. Not a single one of my deaths.

And for that I am grateful.

"I whispered that I loved you and that I would search for you again, until I found you," Cyrus says. His voice sounds tired.

I purse my lips together for a moment, gathering myself. I

wipe the tears from my skin. "Which death was that?" I ask. I don't really want to know. But I do need to piece myself together.

"The sixth," he tells me. "When you wore Edith's face."

Edith. I nod. The recollection of what he says, of being that woman with the blonde hair comes floating through my memory, but only as tangible as fog.

"You never asked me to call you any of their names before," Cyrus says, bringing focus back to me. "Why did you ask me with this one?"

And despite how complicated that answer should be, the answer comes to me, crystal clear, in a single instant.

"Because she, I, wanted you to love her, as just her," I answer honestly. "And because I think, that in some small measure, you did."

He does not say anything. I can feel his turmoil, the struggle inside of himself.

Cyrus' devotion to Sevan is unlike anything this world has ever seen before.

I understand that he cannot admit it. Even to himself. Even to me. Even to Logan. Especially to Sevan.

"I don't know who I am more, Sevan or Logan," I say, finding calm in my voice. "I don't even know who I want to be called. I think it changes moment to moment. I suppose I'm both, and will be until I die again, however soon or far away that might be."

"Don't," Cyrus says, life sparking into his voice again. "Don't say that."

"It's okay," I say hollowly, because I don't really mean it. "I'm only trying to tell you that I want you to think about it.

About your heart. About your truth. Because I'm trying to accept myself, as more than one person. I hope you're one day able to be okay with loving all of the people I am and have been."

"Logan," he says, and a small smile forms on my lips, because he knows exactly who he's talking to in this moment. "I…"

"I just needed to hear your voice," I say, cutting him off. "And I wanted you to know that I do miss you."

The words don't express how badly I do.

"Please," he says, his voice sounding defeated. "Come home."

I shake my head. "It isn't time yet," I tell him. "I'm not ready. And there are still some things I need to take care of."

He's quiet for a moment. I know the struggle this must be for him. He's a man who tells people what to do. He does not have to wait for them.

But he will wait for me.

"Alright," he accepts. "I will continue to try to understand. But Logan?"

My heart skips a beat at hearing him call me that.

"Yes?" I breathe.

"May I please call you?" he asks. "Just from time to time? It's a relief just to hear your voice."

I smile. "Yes, that would be alright."

I can feel it. Clear across the world. Continents apart. His smile.

"I'll talk to you later, Cyrus," I say.

"Goodnight, Logan," he says. And I smile, too.

"Goodnight."

CHAPTER 10

I'VE NEVER BEEN ANYWHERE NEAR THIS FAR EAST, SO IT'S kind of disappointing that I'm doing all this travel, and it's in the dark.

We leave Texas behind, and then cross through Louisiana. The terrain is so flat, it feels weird to me. Like I'm too exposed. I've gotten used to mountains surrounding me my entire life.

"So, are you originally from Mississippi?" I ask Rath.

"I am," he says with a grim nod.

"Then why don't you have a Southern accent?" I ask, teasing just a little.

He looks out the window. "It was part conscious effort, part that most of my communication was with someone who did not have one."

"My grandfather," I say, clarifying.

Rath nods.

"How old are you?" I ask. "And what exactly are you?

Because I can tell you're not a vampire, but you certainly don't smell exactly human?"

"Look at the stones on Logan!" Eshan says from the back seat. "I've been wondering the whole time, but I sure wasn't going to call his species into question."

My face flushes, but really, I want to know.

"I'm old enough to think the world has become a better *and* worse place than it once was," Rath says. "And as for what I am? I am just a man."

"Being vague is your game, I guess," I say with the shake of my head. "Man of mystery."

"My past is complicated. There are some very dark times I went through," he says as he looks out into the dark. "It's a burden I do not feel the need to share with anyone who doesn't absolutely need to know."

I glance over at him.

I think I always knew it. You don't carry around that kind of darkness in your eyes, don't always hold that kind of grim, somber look on your face, without some kind of hardship in your past.

"I understand," I say quietly.

The GPS says we're only an hour away from Silent Bend when Eshan starts breathing hard. I look into the back seat, and see that his eyes have begun glowing a faint yellow.

Suddenly a little burn ignites in my own throat. I swallow once, but the fire grows hotter by the moment.

I haven't drunk since I was in Las Vegas.

"Pull over now," Rath says. "Better you drink farther from the House. It's one of Alivia's rules. If you must drink fresh, you do it far from Silent Bend."

I look over at him, my brows furrowing.

But as I look back at the cooler in the back seat, I see that it's empty.

I take the next exit. And dread forms a thick knot in my stomach when I think about what Eshan and I are about to do.

But my hunting instincts go into overdrive the minute we park in the lot of a gas station.

"If either of us takes things too far, shoot us with those darts," I instruct Rath. With a look in Eshan's direction, I grab the front of his shirt and yank him out of the car.

He was staring at Rath like a meal.

We wait in the shadows, silent. And when a trucker totters out of the side bathroom, I don't hesitate.

I grip him by the front of his shirt, yanking him to me.

My fangs sink into his neck, instantly paralyzing him.

Gross. He tastes like stale nachos and day old donuts.

But the first pull of blood brings a moan from my lips.

Eshan takes his wrist, and sinks his fangs into his flesh.

We're both brand new vampires, Eshan and I. No new vampires have very good control in the beginning.

I know this.

So I was kind of counting on Rath having to use those darts on us.

I'm not surprised, when after six good pulls of the man's blood, Eshan jerks away with a groan of pain.

A moment later, a strong hand clamps down on my shoulder, pulling me firmly away.

I face him, a hiss on my lips, my fangs bared.

But Rath's face is only calm, his eyes determined.

97

"That's enough, Logan," he calmly says. "Leave the man to recover."

I look back at the trucker. His eyes are closed, his head lolled to one side. He's pale, but not deathly so to the point of turning.

I take a breath, telling myself that I took enough to hold me over. Even though my throat still burns. Gently, I drag him to the side of the building. I prop him up there, balancing him so he doesn't fall over.

Rath digs through the trash for a moment, before producing an empty beer bottle. He walks over and stages it in the poor man's hand.

"What if he remembers?" I ask.

"It's doubtful," Rath says. He grabs hold of Eshan and hauls him up and over his shoulder. "And if he does, who would believe him? What proof is there?"

I look back over my shoulder at the poor man as we walk back to the car. I help Rath get Eshan positioned in the back seat and climb into the driver's once more.

"I'm a little tired of having the brain of multiple people," I say as I back out of the space and aim once more for the freeway. "Because this is where Sevan is grateful that there are willing feeders in Roter Himmel. No unwitting victims of our thirst, like that man there. But then Logan is kind of disgusted and baffled that actual humans willingly live in a place like that, where they know they're going to be fed off of, over and over."

"It's difficult to even imagine what you're going through," Rath says.

"So you understand why I wasn't quite ready to return to

Roter Himmel, where everyone expects me to just go back to normal. Where everyone only acknowledges Sevan and expects me to only be her."

I swallow once, thinking of how difficult it's been, every single time. "You understand why I'm not yet ready to go back to the man that did this to me."

"I understand," Rath says quietly.

The miles go by too fast. Louisiana disappears one mile at a time, and it's not long before I see the Mississippi River coming up on the GPS screen. And a moment later, the town name of Silent Bend joins it.

I don't realize I'm holding my breath until my tires hit the enormous bridge that crosses the river and state lines. My knuckles are white as they grip the steering wheel, and I actually have to tell myself not to crush it.

"Alivia has many faults," Rath says as we cross that bridge. "Has made many mistakes. But she is also a good leader. Someone who cares greatly about those that surround her. The tale that Cyrus has told you of her is just one side of the story."

I look over at Rath as we reach the other side of the bridge. And the storm inside of me calms just a little bit.

"Thank you," I say quietly.

I focus on the road before me once again. I try to pay attention. This town is significant to my family, my history.

With the guidance of the GPS, I turn off the highway and onto a road that leads right into the heart of the town.

I enter the main road just by the river. The head of Main Street begins at the water's edge. And there, just before the land falls into the water, there is a gigantic tree. Stones circle it; it sits there like the centerpiece of town. But it's entirely dead. Not a single leaf clings to its blackened branches, despite being the end of July. A shiver works its way down my spine when I look at it.

There's a church, and then another one. A beautiful city building sits on the south side of the road. A few restaurants. A grocery store. And then the schools, elementary, middle, and high.

Then the GPS tells me to turn left, past a few neighborhoods.

My eyes glance down at the screen. One minute until we arrive at our destination.

My heart rate increases. My palms grow sweaty.

Rath glances over at me once.

"Are you nervous, too?" I ask.

"Yes," he admits. "This was my home for a very, very long time. But I have not seen it in sixteen years."

I reach over and take his hand. "Thank you," I say as I glance over at him. "For protecting me all of those years. I know I was just mad at first because I didn't understand who you really were. But thank you. I realize now just how much you sacrificed."

He looks at me. He doesn't say a word. But he nods.

"Arrived," the GPS voice chirps.

And I turn to the left, where Rath points.

A gigantic stone fence wraps around the property, sprawling out in either direction. A huge gate, built with intricate iron, blocks our way. The crest of a raven is set in the center, the name CONRATH inlaid beneath it.

"Do I-" I begin to ask.

"Just wait a moment," Rath says. And then nods his head when the gates slowly begin to open.

My entire body is trembling as I let off the brake and roll forward.

After twenty years of not even knowing the woman's name, I'm finally going to meet her. Face to face.

The grounds are amazing. Gigantic trees line the driveway. Long tendrils of moss hang down from their branches. Flowering bushes are splashed everywhere. The grounds stretch wide and grassy.

But ahead, a house crests into view.

The middle section is white, with gigantic pillars holding the roof up. The wings spanning to the left and right are sided in stone.

It's massive.

And beautiful.

It looks like something out of a fairy tale.

"How old is the house?" I ask, admiring the classic Southern plantation style.

"It was built in 1799," Rath produces the fact without a moment of hesitation.

"Amazing," Logan marvels. There's nothing like this in Colorado. Nothing even close.

Rath directs me to park in front of the garage, which is on the south side of the house. I feel like I'm vibrating as I put the car into park. My entire body is electric. On high alert. Fight or flight.

But still, I climb out. I'm pretty sure my heart is going to pound out of my chest.

Rath takes Eshan and slings him over his shoulder.

And together, we walk up the sidewalk to the massive front porch. I take a deep breath, raising my fist to knock on the front door.

But suddenly it opens.

A woman with tears brimming in her eyes smiles at me.

"Hello, Logan."

CHAPTER 11

A BREATH SLIPS BETWEEN MY LIPS. MY FACE FEELS NUMB. All the blood in my body stops moving.

It's very nearly like looking in a mirror.

That's my jawline. That's my exact nose. Our hair is nearly the exact same shade. Same ears. Same eye shape.

My lips are just slightly fuller than hers. My brow isn't quite as strong. I'm slightly shorter than she is, but with a few more curves.

But everyone has been right.

I look just like her.

And finally, I can't deny it myself.

"You're so young." The words slip out of my mouth before I can think about them.

And she smiles, and a little laugh rushes over her lips.

"I guess there are some perks to immortality," she says, smiling and looking me over.

What I said is true. Alivia Ryan Conrath looks hardly older than myself. Maybe a few years, but not much.

She looks like…like she could be my sister, and the both of us should be heading out for a night on the town.

She doesn't look anything like a woman who has been the leader of a House for sixteen years.

"I…" I shake my head, trying to get myself together. "I mean, I knew you'd been Resurrected for a while, I guess I just had this picture of you in my head. You looked…"

"A lot closer to your mother's age?" she takes a guess.

Her eyes are full of fear, nerves. Her throat is tight, and I can smell the sweat on her palms.

I nod. "I guess."

I finally take a look around, now that the initial shock of seeing Alivia for the first time is over.

The inside of the house is even more beautiful than I expected. A beautiful staircase wraps around the entry and rises to the second floor. Beyond this space, I can see a great ballroom. Ornate carvings are inlaid into the walls. Gold and blue and green are scattered everywhere.

Above us, I find a brilliant, gorgeous chandelier.

It's stunning.

Cyrus' house that he bought back in Greendale was beautiful. But it is nothing compared to Alivia's house.

I realize now that there had been a long, weighted silence, and I look back to my birth mother.

Her eyes are fixed on Rath, who stands beside me with my brother slung over his shoulders.

"Rath," she says in an emotional whisper. "It is so good to see you."

She rushes forward and wraps her arms around the man she sent to watch over me, all those years ago.

Balancing Eshan, he wraps one arm around Alivia, and I see the complicated emotions on his face as he presses his cheek into the top of her head. He squeezes his eyes closed tightly, his lips pressed into a thin line.

They might have a complicated past, whatever it is, just like Cyrus, but it's evident in every inch of his face. Rath loves Alivia. Cares a very great deal for her.

"It is good to be home," he says. And as soon as he says the word, I know he truly means *home* with every single syllable.

There's still so, so much I don't know about Rath.

"I assume this is your brother?" Alivia asks as she releases Rath, looking from Eshan to me.

I nod. "He was turned a few days ago. I…" I shake my head. "I don't even know what to tell my parents. They think he ran off to see some girl he met online. I don't know what he's supposed to tell them when you fix him and he goes back."

"I'm afraid we all have stories to tell when we get involved with this world," she says with a tired expression.

Something sharp and hot spikes inside my chest at her words.

I swallow once, but nod, instead of opening my mouth and spilling vile words.

"I'd love to just sit and…talk," Alivia says, turning hopeful eyes on me. "But I'm sure you're hungry, and tired from a really long road trip," she chuckles just a little. "Why don't we get your brother settled, and then you can eat?"

I nod. I don't speak, because right now I can't sort all my emotions out.

She leads us to a hallway that breaks off to the north. It's long, and I see a dozen doors scattered on either side. She walks halfway down it, and swings it open.

It reveals a beautiful bedroom, decorated in gold and green. A massive bed sits in the middle. Behind it, thick curtains are pulled over the windows, blocking out the light that will soon be filling the world. Off to the left, I see a simple bathroom attached.

"How much longer will he be out for?" Alivia asks as Rath carefully lays him on the bed.

"Another ten or so hours," Rath answers, brushing back Eshan's hair from his forehead.

And I remember, Rath has been watching me, watching my family, for Eshan's *entire* life.

Alivia nods. "We'll come back in a while then, give him the cure while he sleeps, so he doesn't even have to feel the pain."

"Pain?" I ask, my eyes whipping up to hers.

She gives a little nod. "Just for a minute or so. But yes, it does always seem to be painful."

I shake my head. "Rath, you said Cyrus knows about this cure. But he's still outlawed the very existence of the Bitten. I... How did this cure even come into existence?"

A brief look is exchanged between Alivia and Rath. But she looks back at me with confidence and answers in her eyes.

"My sister-in-law, Elle," she offers, "is a brilliant chemist. Back when she was in college, about your age actually, she developed the cure, with the help of another woman. She was risking her own life, helping innocent victims who had been turned. This was several years after Cyrus outlawed the existence of the Bitten. She eventually confessed everything to Cyrus. And he pardoned her. He told her to stop what she was doing, which she did. But we both still have some of the cure. Just for special cases, like your brother."

I swallow once, my throat feeling tight. I understand that risk Elle was taking. How dangerous it is for Alivia to even *have* any of this cure in her possession, considering Cyrus told them to stop.

"Thank you," I say. And that's all I can manage.

Alivia just nods once. She steps out of the room, and Rath and I follow her back down the hall.

We cross the foyer once more, and to the south side. We enter into a beautiful kitchen, where a man works furiously on some food.

He's human. I can smell it.

"Everything is just about finished, Alivia," he says, wrapping things up.

"Thanks, Parker," she says.

"Alivia," Rath asks, looking around. "Where is everyone?"

She looks around, as well. She blushes just a little bit. "I asked the House to give us some space. At least for a few hours, or whenever I tell them they can come back. I thought it might be better to have some time, with just us, before we introduce everyone else."

I nod, grateful.

Alivia gestures to a smaller, informal dining table just to

the side of the kitchen. Awkwardly, I work my way to it, sitting in a chair across from Alivia.

She rests her head in her hand, her elbow on the table, and just looks at me.

My eyes dart away, feeling uncomfortable under her gaze.

"How are you adjusting?" she finally asks.

My chest tightens. My fingers curl into fists in my lap.

I shrug. "It's…it's not easy. But not in a way anyone else can understand."

Her eyes fill with sadness. She gets what I'm talking about.

"How…how long has it been, since you woke up?"

I know she's not just talking about a nap, or a good nights sleep.

"Five nights," I supply.

Her eyes grow wide, her face blanching just a little bit. "Five nights? You…" She shakes her head, a look of respect on her face. "You seem to have some pretty incredible control for it being such a little amount of time. I would have drained Parker in about ten seconds just five nights after I woke up."

She points her thumb over her shoulder at the human man now wrapping things up in the kitchen.

"I had a snack just before we got into town," I say, feeling uncomfortable at the confession.

Alivia lets out another breath though, shaking her head. "Still. Those first few weeks, they weren't easy for me."

I nod, swallowing once. "I guess it's easier, because I knew what to expect. I've done this just a few times before."

She sits back in her seat, her eyes sobering.

Right.

Parker carries over a few platters, setting them on the table before us.

Thick French toast, scrambled eggs. Piles of fruit. A pitcher of orange juice.

And a pitcher of blood.

"Hope you're hungry," Alivia says. Her voice is quiet and tight.

I am actually. My stomach gives a growl, reminding me that I haven't eaten anything since we left Dallas early last night. And even then, it was only an apple and a cheese stick.

I begin dishing food onto my plate.

I glance awkwardly at Rath, and note how stiff and uncomfortable even he seems.

"So, why don't you tell me about yourself, …" she trails off, and it takes me a moment to realize she's questioning what to call me.

No one, not even myself seems to know the answer to that.

"Just…" I shake my head awkwardly. "Just Logan, for now."

"Logan," she says, smiling a little smile. "I'd like to learn more about you, your life. If you don't mind."

I sigh, already tired and overwhelmed.

"I…" Alivia struggles to find the words. "I get it. This is awkward, and weird, and probably way too soon. I don't think either of us was really prepared for this to happen yet. But," she reaches across the table and gently covers my hand with hers. "Here we are."

I look up at her, and I try. I try really hard to piece this woman into the picture I always had of my birth mother. But nothing, not a single bit of her, matches.

Still, I nod.

"I'm guessing you already know some things," I say as I cut into the French toast. "I'm sure Rath has reported plenty of details. Considering he's been watching me for you, most of my life."

Electric and heavy. The air could suffocate us all.

"I…"

But I cut Alivia off. "It's fine," I say around my bite, chewing and speaking at the same time. I feel my Logan-esque defenses rising, the bitter and the bold gathering inside of me.

"I was placed with a family in Greendale," I say. "I don't know how close you lived to there when you…had me."

"A smaller town, about an hour from there," she says, still tense and defensive.

I nod. "My parents names are Gemma and Ethan Pierce. They couldn't have kids of their own. I lived in a nice, red brick house in a quiet family neighborhood my entire life." I stab my fork into a strawberry and pop it into my mouth. "When I was five, my parents adopted my brother, Eshan. He was one. It was a pretty normal childhood."

I look over at Rath, who chews slowly, watching my face the entire time.

"Rath stepped into my life in a public way when I was fourteen," I continue the condensed story of my entire life, the one this woman was never a part of. "He became friends with my parents, and soon he was just always there. Like an uncle and a friend."

I still can't cope with that. The history between us, the family dinners, the laughs at the end of the driveway. The time he helped me study for a US history test. How proud he was when I got my degree.

But I now realize I never really knew anything about him. Who he was? Where he came from? Why he was always there?

"I graduated from high school," I suddenly continue, snapping my eyes back to Alivia. "Then I went to college."

"You have a degree already?" she asks. Her voice is so timid.

I realize she's terrified.

I can't blame her.

There's a lot of aspects about this that are so heavy.

I nod. "Just an associates, which was all I needed for what I went into."

"Which is?" she encourages.

I swallow once.

She knows all of this.

Surely she knows all of this.

Rath has been spying on me my entire life and reporting back to her.

"Mortuary science," I say in a hard voice. My grip on my fork tightens, and instantly it bends to the shape of my fingers.

All eyes snap to it. I release it, and it collapses to the table. It makes a loud clatter, one that rings throughout this entire, huge house.

"I really loved my job," I say quietly. I think back, to the quiet moments in the preparation room. Just me and the dead. They were such good listeners. They all had such great life stories. "I really wanted to work there for a long time."

A quiet, weighted moment follows.

For a moment, I finally get a second to mourn.

My human life. The life I'd worked so hard for.

Gone.

Over.

"I'm so sorry," Alivia says, reaching over once more and placing her hand on mine.

I slide my hand back, tucking it into my lap under the table.

My phone vibrates in my pocket. Grateful for the momentary distraction and release of all this...pressure building inside of me, I pull it out.

I just wanted you to know that I have been thinking about you all night.

And then a second message. *How are you?*

Cyrus.

My heart flutters and I let my eyes slide closed for a moment.

Our moments together, if only connected through this phone, come rushing back to me. The connection I felt. The comfort in hearing his voice. The memories that washed over me. The amount of time I knew he'd spent looking for me. Searching.

My jaw tightens, heat sparks in my chest.

I let my eyes slide open.

Falling on Alivia Ryan Conrath.

"I've heard a lot about you. From the House of Valdez. From Rath. From Cyrus."

The cold in my voice widens Alivia's eyes. She stops breathing and leans back in her chair, her fingers curling into tight fists.

"I heard you knew nothing about your heritage, just like me," I say. That familiar acid rises in my blood. It takes over, turning my vision fuzzy and gray. "But that once you knew your place, you rose to the occasion."

I wrap my hand around the glass of blood. My fingers tighten, and there's a single popping sound as the glass cracks just a tiny bit.

I raise it to my lips, taking a sip.

I enjoy the taste of it as it slides over my tongue. I enjoy the cooling sensation as it slips down my throat. The utter satisfaction as it hits my stomach.

"I haven't heard details," I continue. "But there are certainly legends of your...plots to gain followers. You knew how to read people, how to work them to get what you want."

"Logan-" she begins to defend.

But I continue on.

"I heard you actually married the man who everyone says broke your heart and pushed you to do some very questionable things. You must be a very forgiving person."

"Logan," Rath growls low and dark.

"I guess it runs in our blood," I say. "You forgave Ian Ward, and I keep forgiving Cyrus. The only difference is, Cyrus never turned his back on me."

"You have no idea what Ian has been through," Alivia

says, her voice sparking with defense and anger. "What his family put him through. Ian is a good man."

My eyes harden, just as my heart does. "And what about you, Alivia? Is someone who toys with someone else's heart to console their own broken one a good person? Is someone who kisses a man she's leading on, and could have gotten him killed, a good person?"

Her face is stunned. Frozen in a mask of horror and shock.

"Is someone who left me in the dark, only to let my life be cut short because a member of the House of Valdez recognized me, *you*, and dragged me into this mess, a good person? Is a person who asks someone to live a life of lies for *sixteen* years," I wave a hand in Rath's direction, "a good person?"

Alivia suddenly stands and slaps her hands down on the table. Her eyes ignite red, her expression livid. "Well, this certainly is not how I imagined this moment. You do not know me, Logan. Others can tell the story however they like. But you don't know what me, or my husband, have been through, and the battles we've had to fight to carve out this life for us, and everyone around us. How dare you judge me, us, when you don't really know anything."

"I know that I have *never* seen Cyrus speak with the hardness he does when he talks about you, Alivia," I growl as I, too, stand, staring at this woman across the table. "Cyrus has had many, many enemies over the years, but none have left scars like you have."

She's silent for a moment. I see it in her eyes, she replays whatever happened between the two of them, recalling their past that I really don't want to know anything about.

But they regain their focus, finding me in front of her once more.

"You're right," she says. "I made mistakes. I wasn't kind or careful with Cyrus. I did make him believe. I made him hope. But the King is not innocent in any of this, either."

My blood heats to a boiling point. I feel my fangs lengthen just slightly. "What did he ever do to you?" I'm not quite yelling, but almost.

Rath's hand suddenly darts out, gripping mine.

I look over at him. There's darkness in his eyes. A warning. The truth. He shakes his head just slightly.

Alivia straightens. With cold hardness in her eyes, she reaches up to the neckline of her shirt. She tugs it down, exposing her chest a bit.

She reveals a scar there.

Not just a scar. A brand.

The skin is red and rippled. But I see it there, clear as day. The shape of a crest, a raven set at the center. The exact same as the crest in Rath's ring.

"It's not just what he did to *me*," she says. "But to every member of the House of Conrath."

My breathing comes out hard. I'm wired. I'm an explosive about to set off. A warrior ready to fight to the death over the man I love.

I'm capable of a lot right now. A lot of danger. A lot of blood.

So I do the only safe thing.

I walk away.

But this is not my House. This is not my territory.

I don't know anyone here. I don't know anything about this town. I don't know anything about this entire side of the country.

So I go to the only familiar thing for thousands of miles.

I walk to Eshan's room, and close the door behind me.

CHAPTER 12

Eshan still sleeps on the bed. He looks dead. I have to watch him for a moment to make sure his chest is still rising and falling. When it does, I cross to the bed and sink onto it with a weighted huff of breath.

My phone vibrates again, reminding me that I never actually opened the text message from Cyrus.

I pull it out.

And I just stare at the screen.

And stare.

I don't even know how I am right now, I text.

Almost immediately, Cyrus responds. *What's wrong?*

I pause for a moment, considering how much information to share. Cyrus is known to go overboard. I have to be careful, because I do know he'll do anything for me, anything to protect me.

But he's also the person who knows me best. And I need someone to talk to.

I just met Alivia for the first time, I type out. *Not a single bit of it went how I've always imagined things would be if I ever met my birth mother.*

Oh, he sends as a single word.

That's very big, indeed, he sends after a moment.

That doesn't surprise me though. This is Alivia, after all.

I shake my head and something in my chest tightens. *No, it wasn't even her. It's just…all these memories from other people got into my head. Everything everyone has ever told me. I just…I couldn't even give her a chance.*

I hit send, and I wait for a long minute after it says he's read the message.

To be fair, not everyone is what they seem at first. Reputations do not always encompass the full breadth of a person in reality.

I read his words four times.

He's not just talking about Alivia. He speaks of himself, and my first impression of him.

But these are big words from him. Considering they are spoken about Alivia.

It isn't easy, being that much of an adult, I send him, smiling slightly.

You've always been the better person, he responds. *You've always known what the right thing was.*

His words warm my chest and relieve some of the hot pokers surrounding my heart. I physically feel my muscles relax slightly.

Thank you, Cyrus, I type out.

Always.

I breathe a little sigh as I set my phone beside me on the bed.

All of this is wrong. The timing. The manner. The circumstances.

I'm not good at dealing with these kinds of things.

I look back at my brother and I'm comforted. He would have known I wouldn't handle this very well.

I shift on the bed, climbing up to lay my head on the pillow beside him. I reach up, pushing his hair off his forehead.

A small smile pulls on my lips. And for just a moment, I tell myself that it's all worth it, however this whole trip might go. I'm here because of my brother. And I'll do anything for him.

TIME ALREADY HAS A DIFFERENT MEANING, AND IT'S ONLY been five nights since I became an immortal cursed to die a terrible death.

I have no idea how long I've been lying on the bed with my brother when there's a knock on the door and a moment later Rath steps inside.

I halfway sit up, meeting his eyes.

He stands just inside the door, hands folded in front of him. His demeanor is calm, as almost always. But his eyes. I see how disappointed in me he is. How conflicted he is over everything that has happened since our arrival in Silent Bend, Mississippi.

"We should do this before he wakes up," he eventually says. "As Alivia says, the very beginning is painful."

He walks across the room, crossing to Eshan's side. I see then that he was holding a syringe. Like he's done this before, he uncaps it, pushing out the air bubble. And without one glance in my direction to confirm that this is what I still want to do, he sinks the needle into his arm.

Where once Eshan looked as good as dead, his face winces, just a little. The pain shows in his eyes and in the corners of his mouth.

But just a few seconds later, his expression relaxes again, and once more, he sleeps like the dead.

"How long does it take?" I ask, staring at him.

"Roughly twenty-four hours," Rath says as he recaps the needle and slips the syringe into his pocket.

"And you're sure he'll be human when he wakes up?"

I marvel as I stare at Eshan. I've met and dealt with thousands of Bitten over the years.

But a cure?

"Yes, I'm sure," Rath says.

I look up at him. I study his eyes. I think of his bravery. I think of how much he knows, about everything.

I have to wonder.

But I understand that it's safer, for everyone, that I don't know.

"I know you're mad at me for how things went in there," I say. "I...I honestly didn't know that was going to come out. It just did."

I'm not a person who's very good at being sorry, and honestly, I'm not really sorry now. So I don't say it.

Rath takes one deep breath in and slowly lets it out. He crosses to the chair in the corner of the room, the one that looks like it's at least a hundred years old. He sinks into it, sitting straight. He laces his fingers in his lap.

His eyes are distant, contemplative. He always has words of wisdom, so I allow him a few moments to find them.

"I left Alivia and my service to the House of Conrath just a month after she Resurrected," he begins. "I could not stand by the person she was becoming. I could not support so many of the decisions she was making. Her father asked me to guide her, before he died, and I failed him. Outside circumstances forced her down dark paths and no matter how hard I tried, I could not seem to pull her back onto the straight and narrow."

He crosses one ankle over the opposite knee. "I attended Alivia's wedding, but I cannot say that I ever supported her and Ian's relationship. They are toxic when around one another. The two of them can fight like cats and dogs, fling words that could pierce the thickest armor. Ian told her up front that he would never accept Alivia as a vampire. He used to hunt them. Despite that, she still fell in love with him. Which drove her to do some very dark things when he broke her heart and walked away from her, even though he became what he hated."

Here. Finally. I feel like I'm learning the truth about Alivia. About her husband. Because even though Rath did walk away from her, couldn't support what she was doing, I can still tell. He loves her. Loves her like a daughter, in a small measure.

"Cyrus took Alivia to Roter Himmel for a trial," Rath continues. His eyes flick up to mine. "Did you know that?"

My eyes widen. I shake my head.

Rath nods. "There was an attempt on Cyrus' life, and they staged it to make it look like it was Alivia. Cyrus took her to Roter Himmel and held her prisoner there for over a month. Starved her. Tortured her. He wanted to punish her for how reckless she had been with his heart. He humiliated her. In front of Ian. In front of Raheem."

A small gasp escapes my lips. The spy Cyrus had alluded to that Alivia had gotten involved with. I never... I shake my head. No wonder Cyrus had been so bitter. Raheem had been one of Cyrus' elite, one of his most trusted in thousands of years.

"In the end, their time in Roter Himmel brought Ian and Alivia back together," Rath continues. "Alivia was found not guilty. But she returned to Silent Bend a different person."

I clench my jaw. I'm not ready yet. Not ready to have to accept that that woman, even though she is an immortal, is only human.

"But even though she was changed, I still could not return to her," he says instead.

My eyes narrow at Rath in surprise.

"I couldn't quite forgive Alivia then, and I still don't know that I have yet," he says. "The things she did, the innocent lives she ruined, they're still there. But," he stands, rising to his full height. Rath is a man of power, even though he has lived a life of service. "I do know that time changes people."

He steps forward, toward me. His eyes lock on mine, and

I read the sincerity in them. "It has been sixteen years since I spent time with Alivia. In the immortal perspective of this world, it is not much time, but in reality, it is quite a lot." He reaches forward and takes my hands in his. "I am not asking you to do the same. But I want you to know, that after sixteen years, I am willing to take the time to see if Alivia has evolved into something better than she once was."

He brings my hands up and presses one kiss to my knuckles.

I hold his eyes the entire time, trying to figure out how the hell he's so wise.

I watch as he turns, and walks out the door.

Somewhere in the house, I hear voices. Alivia's. Rath's. Others I certainly don't recognize.

I look over at my phone. Slowly, my fingers crawl over to it, pulling it into my lap.

Words. Cyrus was always very good with words.

He uses them on others. He's used them on me countless times over the years.

He wraps me up. Draws me in. Makes me forget.

Rath's revelation about what Cyrus did to Alivia opens my eyes once more. It reminds me that there is a reason that I am here and not in Roter Himmel with him.

My jaw clenches. My fingers roll into fists.

My blood surges hot.

My fingers wrap around a pillow on the bed, and with every ounce of strength I posses, I fling it across the room with a scream.

It hits the wall and explodes, the cotton flying everywhere.

My fingers slide into my hair, fisting. My breathing comes in and out hard, between my teeth.

I don't know who to trust. No one tells the truth about each other. No one can paint an unbiased picture.

Alone.

Alone, alone, alone.

I feel so damn alone.

And blind.

And insecure.

And unstable.

And in a perpetual state of self-doubt.

Tears prick my eyes, but the anger makes them hot.

I breathe hard, my nostrils flaring.

I turn, feeling lost. Searching for...anything to keep me grounded.

My eyes fall on Eshan. Still in a new state of trans-formation.

Maybe there is one person in this world I can trust. One who unconditionally has my back and doesn't hesitate to give it to me straight. One person who doesn't care about my status as a Queen or eight other people.

But in a few hours he's going to wake up as human again.

And soon I'm going to take him home, and who knows how long it will be until I see him again.

I feel my heart being shredded.

Alone.

I'm going to be alone unless I can turn a blind eye to all the wrongs that are keeping me away from...everyone.

Turning to the back of the room, I cross it. I can feel it outside, the receding of the sun. I feel that utter sense of relief, like lying down after a day of running a marathon. My senses relax. The breath comes to my lungs just a little easier.

I pull the heavy drapes away from the door.

The top half of it is glass, looking out on the darkening world.

I pull it open and step out onto a big, long veranda.

For just a moment, my breath is taken away. Beyond the veranda is a beautiful swimming pool. On the south end of the property, I see a hedge maze, meticulously manicured. Straight out, there is what I think are tombs, a short fence wrapping around them. And beyond the expanse of perfect grass, is the Mississippi River.

Lights flicker on across the water. It's a strange feeling, being this close to a state border, with me standing in Mississippi, and just there where I can see, a whole different life in Louisiana.

I take a deep breath, practically drinking in the humidity. It's hot. Everything about the air feels strange here. So foreign, so different.

I take a step forward, down onto the grass. Through the quiet, I wander around the pool. I stroll toward the river. But right in my way, is that little graveyard.

I read the names as I approach.

Elijah Conrath.

I do remember this name. The heir and ruler of the Conrath family. Faintly, in the back of my memory, I do remember him leaving to sail to the States, with his brother in tow.

Henry Conrath. This tomb is large. Simple but regal. There is no date of his birth or death, only his name. From everything I've learned, he died not long before Alivia came to claim this House.

And then there is Marlane Ryan. She was too young when she died. Only forty-one years old. I note that she died the same year I was born.

Something cracks a little in my chest.

Because I have to tie it all together.

Alivia may be an absolute stranger to me, may feel as familiar as an alien from Venus. But the reality is that she carried me inside of her for nine months. She went through an entire pregnancy and dealt with everything that came with it.

And then her mother died just months before I was born.

I have to think they were close. Alivia was living in Colorado at the time I was born, and before. Her mother would have died in Colorado, I assume. But here she is, at Alivia's House here in Mississippi.

I don't think she would have moved her body all this way unless they were close.

I place a hand on her tomb.

My maternal grandmother.

I look over at Henry's as well, reaching out to touch the warm stone.

My grandfather.

And his brother, my uncle.

"If you want to keep your sanity while trying to puzzle together your family, don't go trying to figure out anything about Henry."

I whip around, all of my senses suddenly coming back as I pull out of my own head.

A woman walks toward me, calm, collected. She doesn't seem scared that I've lowered slightly into a crouch, or that my eyes have ignited brilliant red.

Despite the fact that she is so, so human.

She's medium height, her figure slight. Her hair is blonde. Her features are soft, open. Kind.

I'd describe her as delicate, like a flower.

But there's a certain confidence to her walk. Like she belongs in this world, and knows how to handle herself.

She walks up, and I search her face for familiarities, for clues as to who she is.

She looks to be in her mid-thirties I'd guess.

She's beautiful, but unassuming.

"I didn't know him well, but sometimes reputations and legends *are* pretty accurate."

"What?" I ask, startling as she speaks again.

She bears a Southern accent. And it's kind of adorable on her.

"Henry," she says with a little smiling, nodding her chin toward his tomb.

"Oh," I try to recover, looking back at it awkwardly. "Surprisingly, I haven't heard that much about him. Other than I think I heard Cyrus call him an enemy once."

"Most people only ever see one side of Cyrus," she says calmly. "He's not nearly as unreasonable as some people see him as."

My eyes narrow at this woman and her words, and words spoken over a month ago start rolling through my brain. I try to reclaim them, and the exactness they were spoken in.

"You're Elle Ward, aren't you?" I finally find them.

She offers another small, controlled smile. "Dawes, actually. Have been for the last ten years now."

I nod as the conversation comes back to me. Something about a husband, and…children.

"Aster Dawes," I say, piecing it all together. "Cyrus mentioned a ten-year-old who would be a House leader when she is old enough. And she has a younger brother."

Elle smiles, and I see the pride of a mother in her eyes. She nods. "George. And they have a little sister too, Penny. Aster is here, but the younger two are back home in Boston with their dad."

I didn't realize it was happening. But as she speaks, about something sort of normal—family, I begin to relax just a bit. The tightness in my shoulders calms just a little.

"What's your husband's name?" I ask. "Cyrus couldn't remember."

She smiles, and I swear there's a faint blush that creeps into her cheeks. "Lexington."

I smile, holding in a small, entertained huff at such a strange name.

"So, I guess you're my aunt?" I say, my throat tightening slightly at the word.

Elle shrugs a little shrug. "You can call me whatever you like. I just recognize loneliness when I see it. I thought maybe you could just use a friend?"

I smile hesitantly, but my chest swells with gratitude. Emotion wants to bite the back of my eyes, but I push it back, determined not to cry. "I think I could use one of those right now."

She smiles again. And I think I love her smile. It's always

so small. So unassuming. A hint of uncertainty in it. But it's real. It's supportive and genuine.

"I can't even imagine what you're going through right now," she says, watching my face. "I know the pressure that's on my daughter. But it's nothing compared to what you have. And add all this to the mix?"

She waves a hand toward the House. Through the gigantic windows that lead into the ballroom, I can see people walking around. Other figures move in the bedrooms. Everyone has apparently returned.

"It would be a lot for anyone to deal with."

I nod, continuing to watch the house. "I just..." I shake my head, trying to figure out how to word what I'm feeling. "I don't really know how to trust anyone. There's so much history that I've seen, but the past...hundred years or so seem to have brought around a lot of changes. They seem really important, and I missed a lot. Everyone is trying to fill me in, but I feel like I'm only getting one-sided versions. There's all these new players I have to figure out."

Elle lets out a little sigh. She nods. "I kind of ran away from it all at one point. I needed a break."

"Really?" I say, looking over at her.

She nods. "My grandmother was my guardian for most of my life, and she died when I was sixteen. It was after Alivia and my brother got married, so they took custody of me. I lived here until I graduated high school."

She looks around, and I can only imagine what her life must have been like.

A human girl, living in a House full of beings who would love nothing more than to drain her dry.

"My family has a reputation, too. A really dark one," she says. "After all the drama, after everything everyone knew about me and my family, I left. Went to university. Moved to Boston on my own."

I feel for her. Because after all that effort, here she is again. Mother to an upcoming Royal.

"It's dramatic sometimes," she says, looking over at me. "And beyond stressful from time to time. But it isn't all bad. It brought me my family. My husband was actually a member of Alivia's House for a few years."

My eyebrows rise in surprise, but it does make me smile.

She smiles back. She steps forward and places a hand on my arm. The movement is comforting. "Logan," she says. Her words are soft. "It's okay to not be okay. And anyone who doesn't get that right now just doesn't matter."

A flood of relief washes through me.

It's okay to not be okay.

Emotion does push its way to the surface now. Tears pool in my eyes, but don't quite break free. I bite my lower lip as I take a step forward. I wrap my arms around this precious woman, and for the first time, I feel it.

A connection.

A bond.

To my family.

"Thank you," I breathe. "Thank you so much."

"You're welcome," she says. She actually runs a hand down the back of my head, smoothing it over my hair.

I release her, taking a deep breath as I wipe the tears from my eyes. I smile when Elle looks at me.

"I have to admit, I'm a little embarrassed to go back in

there and face Alivia again," I say with a little laugh. "I threw a bit of a tantrum earlier."

She laughs, too. "I think she'll get over it. If one is all she ever has to deal with, I think she'll survive."

The look in her eyes tells me the story of the past ten years of being a mother to three.

I laugh again, grateful for this woman's insight and finesse. With a sigh, I look back toward the house.

"Stay with me?" I ask. Because I really am scared.

"Of course," she says. And she slides her hand into mine.

CHAPTER 13

TOGETHER, WE WALK BACK ACROSS THE GROUNDS, AND through the doors into the ballroom.

Inside, I see a man, a look of focus on his face as he heads from the kitchen toward the bedrooms. But when he sees us, he does a double take, instantly stopping in his tracks.

"Well, hello, Logan," he says dramatically. He saunters over, his eyes stripping me down.

"I'm a little taken," I say with snark. "I'd be careful if you know what's good for you."

He smiles, as if undeterred. Elle laughs.

"Logan, this is Christian Kask," she introduces the man. "And this isn't really flirting. It's just the Kask way."

His smile grows even more flirtatious as he extends a hand for me to shake. "Pleased to make your acquaintance."

I smirk at him, shaking my head, but take his hand.

He's good looking. That's for certain. But he's a player, through and through.

"Trust me, there are too many reasons for me to not lay the real charm on," he says with a smile.

"Oh?" I question, raising an eyebrow. "And what are those?"

He smirks, and I can totally see how he operates. That charming smile, those bedroom eyes…

"One," he begins. "There's the fact that you look so much like Liv. Don't get me wrong, Liv is a beautiful woman, and I certainly would have banged her in the beginning."

I fix him with a look, but he only smiles again.

"But she's family, has been for a long time." And now I see the genuine spark in his eyes. "And then, two: your husband had my father killed, pretty brutally, a long time ago."

Bam.

Smack me in the face.

My blood chills and I feel my expression slacken.

"Don't worry, doll face," Christian says. "You didn't do it."

I don't know what to say or how to react. But thankfully I'm saved when someone else walks into the ballroom.

"So this is the woman who put Mom and Dad into such a tizzy."

The man looks terrifying. Honestly.

His hair is bleached blond-white, but his features are sharp, hawk-like. His eyes are dark. His lips set in a thin line. I'm pretty sure he could cut me clean through with his gaze.

But he smiles this…smile. Wicked and gleaming.

Mom and Dad…he certainly doesn't look like he should be calling them that. He looks like he's close to forty.

"If you have any issues with my presence, you can file an official complaint to Roter Himmel," I say, straightening, fixing him with my own gaze.

The look in his eyes changes, and his smile does, too.

"It is a pleasure to finally meet you, my Queen," he says, bowing deep before me. "I've heard so much about you."

I stand straight, tall. Rising above and reminding myself of who I am.

"Wow, Smith," Christian says. "Think you can grovel any deeper?"

Smith looks over to Christian, his eyes darkening. "She may be Alivia's daughter. And she may look like she should be in high school. But I will not forget who she really is, mate. I don't see the harm in showing respect to the Queen who rules over us all."

Christian's expression falters. His eyes slide over to me, and look doubtful, maybe slightly fearful. And he tips forward in an awkward little bow.

Over the other noises of the house, my ears pick up on voices. Upstairs, to the north end of the house.

They're yelling.

My brows furrow.

"Like I said, you put Mom and Dad in a tizzy," Smith says, raising one eyebrow.

I look over at Elle in confusion.

"I think Alivia told Ian that your first meeting didn't go quite as expected," she says. "This," she waves a hand in their direction, "is just how they communicate sometimes."

"And somehow they've stayed married?" I question.

"They say make up sex is the best sex for a reason," Christian says.

"Seriously?" Elle yells at him, her brows furrowing in annoyance. "That is my *brother*."

He just shrugs and chuckles.

"The way those two fight every other week, it must be truly great," Smith says as he tucks his hands into his pockets. He turns as if to leave. "If you need anything, you let me know, my Queen."

There's dark devotion in his eyes when he says it. And I can tell he means it.

"Thank you," is all I can give him.

As he walks out of the ballroom, I see two faces poke around the corner. Nervous whispers find their way to my ears.

"It's okay," Elle says, sounding slightly exasperated. "You two can come out."

Around the corner, two women nervously walk out. Their eyes are bright, they don't seem to know what to do with their hands, and they're giggling and giddy.

"Is...is it really true?" the first asks. But she directs her question at Elle. "The Queen has really returned?"

Elle looks at me, and raises an eyebrow.

"It is," I say, feeling exasperated.

This is freaking exhausting sometimes.

They both let out a loud squeal, one of them actually jumping up and down.

"This is seriously so exciting," the other says. "We have heard stories, and oh, it's just so tragic and romantic. I loved hearing about you and Cyrus when I was a kid."

"Where is he?" the other asks. "Are you two planning a big wedding again? I can't even imagine how amazing it must be to be together again after so long!"

"Girls," a firm but gentle voice says. I look past them and see a man step into view. He wears a blue suit. Extremely light strawberry blond hair sits atop his head. "Give your greetings to Logan, and let her be."

They give me another excited look and squeal. "I'm Stephanie," one pipes up as she enthusiastically shakes my hand. "Nikki," the other says, making a breathy little sound when she shakes mine. "If you need anything, we're your girls."

With more squeals and giggles, they both scamper away.

"That was delightful," I say as I watch them go.

The man crosses the ballroom. "I apologize for them," he says. He's British, immediately given away by his accent. "I guess there's been too much anticipation for them since they learned of your arrival a few days ago."

He stops in front of me. His ice blue eyes are inquisitive, but they are kind. Open.

"It is a pleasure to meet you, though, Sevan," he says as he takes a little bow in front of me. "After all this time… It's an honor."

"Please," I blush. "Just…call me Logan, for now."

"Logan," he concedes with a little tip of his head. "I am Nial Jarvis. Welcome to the House of Conrath."

"Nial is a doctor," Elle continues the introduction. "He

supplies pretty much everyone here with donor blood. And he takes charge of the House whenever Alivia has to travel."

"I do what I can for Alivia," Nial says. There's a certain humility about the man. It's refreshing. "She is family to me."

Family.

There's that word Edmond kept using when talking about the House of Conrath.

"It's nice to meet you, Nial," I say. And I actually mean that.

The fighting upstairs winds down, the words coming fewer and farther between. All our eyes rise to the ceiling when we hear a door open.

My heart jumps into my throat.

I hear footsteps, just one set of them, walk through the halls upstairs. And then I hear them pad down the stairs.

And then a moment later, Alivia rounds into the foyer.

We stand there for a long moment, just looking at each other.

"I know you've gotten what you came for," she says quietly. "But please, Logan. Will you please stay for a while?" There's emotion in her voice. She keeps control over it, though. Just barely. "Can you please...can you please give me a second chance?"

I swallow once, because it's the only way to get my heart back under control. Tentatively, I take one step forward. My eyes rise from the floor, up to her face.

"I..." I sigh. I really don't know how the hell to say what I feel. "I shouldn't have freaked out on you like I did earlier. I wasn't being fair. I..." My voice trails off again, and I feel a little hollow inside. "I'm kind of a mess right now."

I still don't apologize. But it's the best I can do right now.

She crosses the space, and stops just a few feet in front of me. Slowly my eyes rise up to hers again.

"That's okay," she says. "In case you haven't noticed yet, we're all kind of a mess here."

An emotional, appreciative laugh huffs out of my lips. And I finally let her, as Alivia wraps her arms around my back and hugs me.

I hesitate. I shouldn't. I never imagined I would. But I stand there for several long seconds with my arms hanging at my sides.

It's all different.

Every bit of it.

Different than I ever imagined.

But it's okay to not be okay.

To not be how I imagined.

For things to be different.

Finally, I raise my arms, and wrap them around my birth mother.

I let my eyes slide closed. I press my face into her hair. The hair that is the same shade as mine. I hug her frame that is slighter than my own, and also a little taller. But as my heart beats in my chest, it tells me the truth.

We have our similarities. We have our major differences.

But this is the woman who carried me inside of her for nine months. This is the woman who didn't abort me, whatever the circumstances were in the beginning. It's the woman who did what was best by knowing there was another family who could give me a better life than she could.

Thank you, the thought rolls through my head.

I can't voice it. Because I'm the same salty Logan I was a week and a half ago.

But I can admit it to myself.

"Second chances," I say instead.

Alivia hugs me tighter for a moment before releasing me. She smiles, appreciation and emotion shining in her eyes.

Footsteps on the stairs draw my eyes back to the entryway. Alivia turns as well, and we both see as a man rounds the stairs and turns toward the ballroom.

There's hardness in his eyes. Doubt. Questioning. His lips are pressed into a thin line and his jaw is tight.

I know exactly who this is and what he and Alivia were just fighting about.

He doesn't like me.

Ian Ward is medium height, but his body is honed. Muscled arms, a broad, thick chest. Various scars line his arms. His brown hair is quite a bit lighter than Alivia's. He's attractive. In a backwater, rugged type of way.

"Logan," Alivia says. There's a stubborn tone to her voice and she lifts her chin just slightly. "This is my husband, Ian."

I hear him let out a hard breath through his nose. His left hand curls into a fist and the set of his lips thins out even more.

Ian Ward is hot-headed. I've not even spoken a single word to him and I can already tell.

But he takes a step forward, and then another to cross the

ballroom. He extends a hand. I make sure I stare him down, show him that I don't give a damn what he thinks of me, as I shake his.

"It's a pleasure to meet you, Ian," I say. I want to add, *I've heard a lot about you*, because I have, but I'm trying to be mature and act like the Queen I'm remembering. So I keep the words sealed, safe and sound, behind my lips.

"Logan," is all he says, an acknowledgement. He stares me down.

But I see a warring of emotions. Anger. Distrust. But also…reverence.

"I guess you've already met some of the House members," Alivia says, placing a hand on my shoulder and turning me away from her distrusting husband. "And Elle."

I nod. "I totally get why she's Cyrus' favorite," I say with a wink in her direction. "And Christian was very…friendly. And then there was Smith."

Alivia gives a little smile and chuckle, as if she totally gets why I didn't have a word to say more about him.

I'm still not sure how to take him.

"Do you mind if I introduce you to everyone else?" she asks, her eyes unsure. "We were about to eat dinner."

I nod.

Time to stop being a baby.

I've met thousands of new people throughout my lives. I've dealt with people who wanted to kill me. People who cursed my name.

I can handle Alivia's House.

"It's dinner time!" Alivia says, raising her voice. With a smile, she holds her hand out toward the formal dining room.

Side by side, we walk in. She sits at the head of the table. Ian sits beside her, and I take the seat on her other side.

Ian keeps watching me. His eyes bore into me, as if he can read what kind of a person I am off my skin.

I only offer him a polite look every now and then.

Christian immediately follows us, Stephanie and Nikki aren't far behind, with more whispers and amazed looks in my direction. Nial sits at the other end of the table, shooting the women annoyed glares that yell *get a grip*.

Three more women wander in, all of them fierce looking. Rath joins a moment later. And that sets everyone into words of surprise and welcome home.

And then Elle comes around the corner, and walking next to her, is a young girl.

My heart flutters.

She's young. So, so young.

Ten years old.

But here she is, human as her mother at the moment. She walks with confidence, and it's obvious she knows what all of us are. But she's not afraid. She looks absolutely comfortable and at ease.

Her hair is blonde, but as the light hits it, I swear I see the faintest trace of strawberry in it. Her nose is tilted up just a tad, her cheeks are just beginning to lose the roundness of baby padding.

She looks a lot like her mother.

She's precious.

I scoot my chair out and turn to her, rising to my feet.

"Aster, this is Logan," Elle says. "She's aunt Liv's daughter."

Aster gives me a shy smile, looking me up and down. "You look just like aunt Livy."

I smile. "That's what everyone says."

"My friend Annika was adopted," she says. "But she got to see her first mom lots. It would have been nice if you could have done that, too. I always wanted cousins."

Both Elle and Alivia make noises, to stop her, or just noises of surprise.

"You know, that would have been nice," I say with a smile. I reach out and she takes my hand. "I had cousins on my adopted dad's side, but they lived really far away in Virginia so we only got to see each other every other year or so. But I think it would have been nice to spend time with you, too."

Aster smiles. And my heart cracks.

She's so sweet. Just like her mom.

"I heard my other cousin is sleeping," she says. "When will he wake up so I can meet him, too?"

A little chuckle bubbles up from my chest, and I smile, my entire soul warming. "I've never done something like this before, but I've been told he'll be awake in about twelve hours. I'm sure he'll be excited to meet you."

Aster Dawes smiles, big. Showing off two missing teeth.

I smile and look up at Elle.

And just then, I think my heart grows three sizes.

Elle guides her to a seat, and everyone sits as the cook and another woman bring dishes to the table. The room fills with the scent of food, and my mouth waters.

"I'll admit," I say as I begin dishing up food, after Christian starts us off. "I've heard talk about the House of Conrath from Cyrus, Rath, the House of Valdez. It's smaller than I expected."

"This is only a third of us," Alivia says. "Eight are in Florida at the moment, dealing with a few small issues. And the others are in the region, keeping things in check. In all, there are twenty-six in the House of Conrath."

I look around the table. Christian, Nial, Smith, Stephanie, and Nikki.

"Oh," Alivia says. "Right, you haven't met quite everyone. Logan, this is Pearl," she says pointing to a woman with dyed silver hair. She gives me this little two-fingered salute. "And Leigh. She's our acting attorney."

Leigh is curvy and dark and beautiful. She offers a little smile.

"And Anna," Alivia says, nodding toward the woman sitting beside Nial. Dark brown hair and pouty lips make her beautiful. "She's my head of security."

Anna doesn't give me more notice than one little look in my direction.

"And everyone, you already know, but this is Logan," Alivia says awkwardly.

"Also known as Queen of all vampires," Leigh says. But her tone is impressed, in a *go girl* kind of way. She winks at me.

I sigh. I really don't know how to deal with all this attention.

"Pretty impressive," Anna says as she dishes her food. "The fact that Alivia hid that you exist from all of us for sixteen years."

"They didn't…" I trail off, looking toward Alivia.

She shakes her head. "No one knew," she says. "Except for Rath and Ian."

I nod. I'm not sure how to process that.

"Food," a voice suddenly says from outside the dining room. It echoes around the foyer, throughout the house, and I actually jump. "I smell food."

A boy wanders into the dining room. He looks young, slightly younger than myself. Sandy blond hair. His eyes are slightly bloodshot.

He walks in wearing nothing at all except a pair of boxers.

"Cameron!" Alivia says in part horror, part humor. "I think you're forgetting something."

He looks around, as if confused. And then with an expression of cleverness, like he's just figured it out, he grabs the last plate from the table. He nods his head in her direction and winks.

He's high. No doubt about it, he's high.

I can smell the pot on him.

I take every bit of this in in just a second.

But none of it matters. Because my eyes lock on his bare chest.

The word TRAITOR was carved into his skin at some point. It's now healed into red and white scars, but there the words are, big and bold and roughly hewn into his very skin.

Just below that, there's the Conrath crest, burned into his skin. Just like Alivia's.

This Cameron was tortured.

"Tell me where he is," Cyrus seethed. He held the glowing metal blade just to the side of the man's face. I could

smell his skin begin to smolder, the hairs on his face burning. He hissed in pain, his face contorting with it.

"I told you, as far as I know he was killed twenty years ago," the man pleaded. He struggled against the guard, fighting to get away from the branding that was coming that would permanently mark his face.

"Oh, but he apparently was not," Cyrus hissed next to his ear. "For three of my men were found down by the lake, decapitated, their scalps removed. No other kills one of us in that manner. So tell me, where is he?"

"I told you, he's dead!" the man screamed.

Cyrus gave a bellow and pressed the glowing blade to the side of his face. I winced as I looked away.

I hated this. Every second of it. The levels Cyrus would resort to...

But I could not stop it.

Not when it was over something this important.

But the man's screams...

"Just because he is dead does not mean it wasn't one of the others!" the man sobbed. "There were *three* of them that you did not kill. I told you, this one is dead, but there are still two others it could be."

"No," Cyrus growled. "There aren't. For the other two reside in the depths of these walls."

The man's eyes slowly rose up. "Are you sure about that?"

The uncertainty crept into Cyrus' eyes.

Before they filled with anger and disgust.

He sliced up the man's middle, and all of his internal organs spilled onto the stone floor.

CHAPTER 14

As dinner winds down and House members drift off, Alivia touches my shoulder and inclines her head toward the door. My heart rate immediately skyrockets into my throat, my palms sweat, and I start an internal lecture about not making an ass out of myself again.

I follow Alivia out the door and slowly we start walking over the grounds.

"I hope they all weren't too overbearing," Alivia says with a little smile.

I smile too, shaking my head. "They were just fine. I really like Elle, and Leigh. Even Christian, I think."

She laughs at that.

"But, I don't know that Ian is ever going to like me much," I add, sobering my tone.

Alivia sighs. Her eyes wander over the property, as if searching for words to form an explanation. "Ian is…stubborn. He gets kind of set in his ways and a change of mind isn't easy for him."

I bite my lower lip, stuffing my hands into my pockets. "Not that I care if he likes me, because honestly, I really don't. But is it just because of...our first conversation?"

She looks over at me. "In part."

But her eyes are holding back so much information.

"What's the other part?" I ask.

She offers a sad smile. "We'll get to that later."

A white gazebo comes into view and Alivia heads for it. Two cute swings hang from the edges, looking out over the river. Alivia sinks onto one, so I sit too, a large gap between us.

"I'm really glad you have a brother," she says through the comforting dark. "I was an only child, and it was lonely. I always wanted siblings."

"Eshan can be a punk sometimes," I say with a huff. "But I love him. Even though we came to our parents in very different ways, from different parts of the world, we still get each other."

Alivia nods.

She's quiet, and I can feel the thoughts rolling through her head. Digging through the past. Sorting through the present.

"I'd like to know," I finally say when she says nothing. "About the beginning. The...circumstances leading up to me becoming a Pierce."

Alivia bites her lower lip, just as I did a minute ago.

Maybe we're more alike than I realized.

"I guess it starts with my beginning," she says. Her eyes

fall to her lap, where her fingers lace together. "My mom grew up in Mississippi. She was here in Silent Bend, working for the summer after her first year of college. She met my father one night and they bonded. It was just a one-night thing, though. Their paths never crossed again. My mother was going to school in Colorado; she wanted to become a veterinarian. So at the end of the summer, she went back, and a few weeks later, realized she was pregnant with me."

She's barely even begun, but already she's making my heart ache for her.

"She never told Henry about me," Alivia says. She looks up, her eyes looking over the river, but not really seeing anything. "She was determined to do this on her own. And she did. She was a great mother, more than I probably deserved." She smiles, her eyes going soft. "But it was hard. She dropped out of school and worked at the same diner my entire life. She'd work these crazy long hours, just to pay the bills. We lived in five different tiny apartments over my life. She was always so stressed."

She swallows, her eyes falling back to her lap.

"But I didn't really mind. I told myself that material things didn't matter, and really, I was okay with it all. But I felt kind of guilty, you know? Like, because I came along, I held her back." She gives this little shrug.

"I'd been dating this boy most of my senior year of high school, but we broke up two weeks before graduation. So, when I met this guy at the end of summer break, and he was so sweet and attentive, I jumped in to try to patch myself back together."

She grows very still. Very quiet.

"It wasn't fair of me, but I'd always judged my mother a little bit, for getting pregnant when she was still just a kid, had no idea what she was really doing." Her voice grows tight, her voice a little hoarse. "And there I was, even younger than she was, pregnant. And I didn't know a thing about the father."

My own throat grows tight. I blink five times fast.

No one knows. No one has known who my father is.

And here's the account, from my own mother's lips, about him.

"I was scared out of my mind," Alivia continues. "But I was going to do it. I was going to raise you. Mom was going to help me. She had done it, and I had turned out happy and healthy, so I was determined I could do it, too."

Emotion thickens her voice. She stops talking and the thickness of the air doubles.

"And then she died," I say. My eyes drift back toward the family graveyard. To where I stood before her tomb.

Alivia nods. A single tear slips down her face.

"I was wrecked," she says. "She was walking home from work. This girl…she was on her phone, she ran the light." She shakes her head. "I couldn't… I didn't know what to do. My mom was all I had. The only family I knew. I kind of shut down." She holds her stomach and the breath stills in her chest.

"I couldn't even take care of myself," she says. "I knew I had no place taking care of a baby." More tears roll down her face. She covers her mouth with her hand.

My chest hurts. It hurts to breathe. To move. To exist.

I feel Alivia's pain in every inch of me.

"I did what I thought was best for you," she says finally. "Let you have a family. Not just a broken kid. It was the hardest thing I'd ever done. But I knew it was the right thing."

She doesn't look over at me, as if she can't handle the answer in my eyes if it was the right thing or not.

I'm not always a nice person. But I can't just let her sit in uncertainty and agony.

"You did the right thing," I say. I begin to reach over, contemplating touching her hand. But I can't yet. "My parents are great. My dad is enthusiastic and on board with everything. My mom's whole life was about me and my brother. I had a great life with them."

She smiles, and finally, looks up at me.

Her eyes are filled with tears. But there's hope in them.

"Thank you," she offers.

We both look back out over the river. Only a few lights are still on now. It's the middle of the night, the darkest part.

"You were three when I found out about Henry Conrath and moved here," she continues the story. "When I came here, and everyone tried to use me and manipulate me." She abruptly stops. She looks down in her lap again, shaking her head.

I hadn't really stopped to consider it. What Alivia was walking into. How hard that must have been. When she had known nothing about this world, and was suddenly expected to be a leader.

But I see it now, in the eyes of every one of those House members. They respect Alivia. They love her. Even Edmond said they had died for one another and would do it again.

"I'd never been in love before I met Cyrus," I say. My heart is racing. But I have to ask. "Before I died. So I guess this is the part I've struggled with the most. Everyone has had all these things to say about you. But so much of it is about your romantic relationships. I hate to ask you to explain yourself, but can you please help me understand? Can you please tell me the truth?"

She looks over at me, and I see it there in her eyes. She knows she made mistakes. And she can't believe my opening statement.

"These are not short stories," she says. "There's so much history, back story. But there's nothing wrong with asking for the truth."

She tucks her knees up to her chest, wrapping her arms around them. "Ian and I should never have fallen in love. We were bound to be enemies from the time we were born. I had my heritage, and at the time, he thought vampires had killed both of his parents," she begins. "So, he was very up front with me, that we could never be together, once I had Resurrected." The distance in her eyes tells me how hard that must have been at the time. "But, we fell in love, anyway. And then, early on, someone who wanted my House killed him, right in front of me."

Enemies. There are always enemies in our world, no matter if you are a Born, a Royal, or the King of them all.

"But four days later, Ian came knocking on my door, Resurrected as a Born," Alivia says. "His mother had an intentional affair and conceived him, but he never knew. And Ian just couldn't accept himself. He hated everything about himself, and everything I was about to have to embrace."

"You knew Cyrus was coming," I say. "Once word got out about a new female Royal, he would have been very eager to see you die."

Just as he had me, just a month and a half ago.

Alivia nods.

"The tension leading up to Cyrus' arrival drove the wedge between Ian and I even deeper. And finally, it got to be too much. We called it off, dark, bitter words were said. And we ended things."

She toys with the hem of her shorts, picking at a thread there.

"During that time, Cyrus had sent a spy to watch me," Alivia moves on. "Raheem. He eventually came into the light. Over a few weeks, we got to know one another. In him, I saw darkness that I recognized in my own heart. He encouraged me to accept my fate, to embrace the life I was born to be. Raheem accepted me and never once resented who I was."

Acceptance.

It's what we all need.

And I begin to understand.

Raheem gave her what Ian never could.

"But he kept his distance," Alivia says. She looks up. "He knew the weight of Cyrus' arrival and the potential for what could happen after I resurrected. It continued to rip me to pieces, my heart. I knew I didn't love Raheem, but in a way, I needed him just to breathe."

I try to recall his face. Raheem. Dark skin. Dark eyes. Mysterious, and a child of the desert.

But it's been a long time.

"And then Cyrus arrived, and the end of my life came," my mother continues to tell her story. "There is something to be said about Cyrus. He's captivating. He's intriguing. He's intense. I didn't expect that." She shakes her head.

"The way he looked at me. The hope and longing in his eyes."

She looks over at me. "I wanted to be you," she says softly. "I wanted to end that pain in his eyes. I wanted to remember a past life so that I could forget the pain in my chest. So I could move on. Whenever I was with Cyrus, I desperately wanted to be you."

Everything she says about Cyrus is true. He is engrossing. He holds a power over people.

Without even realizing it, he put a spell on Alivia.

I know it now; she never really stood a chance.

But Alivia Ryan Conrath is capable of far more than she looks.

Cyrus didn't stand one either.

"I knew I was playing with fire," Alivia confesses. "That I shouldn't do what I was doing. Shouldn't let Cyrus hope. But I wanted it. I also wanted to make the pain stop. Because there was Raheem, waiting in the shadows, soft touches and stolen kisses. There was Cyrus, looking at me with so much longing. But all I wanted was Ian."

Her voice grows breathy. Quiet.

The two of them are toxic. I have spent hardly any time around the two of them, but I can already tell. They're toxic around each other.

But we all have our brands of acid. Maybe they are the only two who could mix with one another.

"I didn't mean to break Cyrus," she says, looking over at me. "And I regret what I did, every day."

I swallow and my eyes drop away from hers for a moment.

Everyone does things that they regret.

And I've heard more stories.

I think I understand now, another reason Ian will never like me. I'm married to the man who tortured his wife. Ian has only ever seen the dark side of Cyrus, only has a few years of history and a limited set of experiences with him.

I can tell: Ian is a man who does not forgive.

"Rath said Cyrus held you at Roter Himmel, and I've seen the brands," I say quietly. "I..." I trail off, shaking my head. "I don't know that I want to hear those stories. I know what Cyrus is capable of. How big of a grudge he can hold. So I think it's safe to say that you're probably even."

She gives a little huff, and I see it in her eyes. Not even close.

I wonder again, just what exactly did Cyrus do to Alivia while she was at Roter Himmel?

"Well, at least one good thing came out of it, well, two I guess, since it was our time there that brought Ian and I back together," she corrects herself. "But that's where I saw your father, and knew he was a Royal."

I look back at her. "So you do know who he is?" My heart plunders my body, raging.

She shrugs. "I recognized him, but I never spoke to him. I knew he hadn't given me his real name all those years ago. And I was terrified. What were the chances that I, a Royal who didn't even know she was a Royal, would sleep with another Royal?"

"Slim to none," I say, my brows furrowing. "Alivia, do you think that somehow he knew what you were?"

She shakes her head. "I don't know, but it just can't be coincidence, it just doesn't seem realistic."

I nod. The odds...

"So you don't know his name?" I ask. She shakes her head. "But if you were to come to Roter Himmel, you would be able to identify him again, right?"

Her face pales. I understand. Not many come to Roter Himmel under positive circumstances. And if she was there so Cyrus could get revenge... Asking her to go back is big.

"I could," she says. Her voice is tight. "And I will. If you want me to."

I offer her a small, appreciative smile. "Maybe. I'll have to think about it. This is all...everything. It's just happening so fast. Just a month ago I was worrying about money problems, and now I'm..."

Alivia reaches over and places a hand on my knee.

"Please," she says, and her tone makes me meet her eyes again. "I know you've been through a lot. But ever since I realized, I knew, that you would be the one, when you were just four years old, I tried to keep you out of this, for as long as I could. Can you...can you please tell me what happened?"

I look at her for a long moment, my eyes flicking to hers, one and then the other.

This is our biggest difference. Our eyes.

I did not get them from her.

"Rath and I had had a fight," I begin. "There had been some attacks in the area—vampire. He wanted me to move back in with my parents, I told him that was never going to happen. Anyway..." I shake my head, remembering the annoying night. "We stumbled upon two vampires dealing with the attacker. It was a mess. Rath begged them to let us go, but the man, he kept looking at me and demanding to know who I was."

Realization creeps into Alivia's eyes.

"I look a lot like you," I say softly. "And finally he realized it. He probably would have let it go, considering I was the daughter of a female Royal, but with Rath there..."

Alivia sighs. "In the end, the man I sent to protect you was the one who gave you away."

I nod. "Cyrus arrived just hours later," I say. "Tested my blood, confirmed I was Royal through both lines. He wanted to kill me, right then and there."

"How the hell did you ever stop him?" she asks.

I laugh. "I made a deal with him. He could kill me, but he had to give me a month to wrap up my human life. And he had to get to know me during that month. My intent was that it would change his mind and he would decide that I didn't have to die."

Sadness creeps into her eyes. Heavy. Regretful.

"So I assume your month ran out," she concludes.

But I shake my head. "Someone tried to kill him. I stopped them, but it cost me my own life."

Alivia angles toward me, leaning in closer. The moment grows heavier. Denser.

"And what made you do that, Logan?"

I look up, my eyes rising to the stars above us. I search them, trying to remember everything I know about them. So that I can know which same ones Cyrus might be looking at.

"You said you'd never been in love before you met Cyrus," Alivia says softly. "You didn't say that as Sevan, did you?"

I take a few more breaths, still staring at the stars. Slowly, I let my eyes slide closed. I feel his breath on my neck. I imagine his lips. I hear the sound of him humming.

"No, I didn't," I answer.

She lets me sit in the quiet for a few moments, just lost in thought. In my own memories.

A helicopter ride.

A fake bowling date.

His hand in mine.

Looks across my parents' kitchen table.

A kill defending my honor.

The look of guilt in his eyes.

"It's kind of annoying, isn't it?" Alivia says eventually. "When our hearts want something that logically seems so bad for us?"

A little chuckle escapes my lips. I open my eyes and look back at Alivia, who smiles back, and I realize, she does get it.

She sighs. "I'm sorry all of it, every piece of this, is such a mess," she says. "But I'm really glad you're here. And I'm really glad we're getting this time."

I smile. "Me too," I say. "None of it is how I thought it would be, someday. But we roll with the drama, don't we?"

She smiles. "I guess it's what we do."

CHAPTER 15

I'M MENTALLY DEPLETED BY THE TIME I WALK BACK INTO Eshan's room an hour before the sun will come up. It's been an incredible day, but so draining.

I've just taken my shoes off and changed into comfortable clothes, about to climb into the bed, when my phone starts vibrating.

Larkin's name displays across the top.

With my heart jumping into my throat, I step out onto the veranda and answer.

"Larkin," I say breathily. "What have you found?"

"I've been watching the house since I arrived in town," he immediately reports. "No one has been here since."

"So, if there were any other players involved besides the one Cyrus killed, they've moved on," I say, my stomach sinking. Who knows where they'll go from here.

"I don't think so, Sevan," he says. "There have been two cases of animal attacks at the hospital. The victims don't remember anything, but they have bite marks and were missing a lot of blood."

I sink into a chair. My face feels cold suddenly. "So someone is still in the area. But how would they not know Cyrus has left?"

"They could think he's gone just temporarily," Larkin speculates. "Or perhaps these attacks are separate."

"Somehow, I doubt it," I say. I straighten in my seat, holding the phone to my ear. "Either way, I think it's time to get the House of Valdez involved."

"I called them just before I called you," he says. "They will arrive in a few hours."

I nod. "Good. Something with this still doesn't sit right, Larkin. It was an attack on Cyrus, but it was weak. Almost as if they were only testing something. I just don't know what, yet."

"I will, my Queen," he says, and then ends the call.

I turn and walk back into the bedroom. Silently, I stare at my phone, tapping it on my hand as I consider for several long minutes.

There are people I care about that are still in Greendale.

Amelia. Tanner. Emmanuel. My parents are in the next town over, but not far.

Just a month and a half ago, it was a serial killer who was shredding women and decapitating them. This was only two people bitten, but the danger is still very real.

I sit in the chair in the corner, still staring at my phone.

We do this, over and over. Bite innocent people. Take their blood.

I picture Amelia, puncture marks in her neck, her eyes

staring vacantly at the ceiling. I picture my mom, stone white, never to offer me a smile again.

I walked into the room, and the smell of it hit me before my eyes could register what was happening.

Blood.

I smelled blood.

And there was the man lying on the floor, blood running from his neck, spilling onto the floor. Four puncture marks sank deep into his skin.

"Hel…" he struggled for breath. "Help me."

Fear set his eyes wild.

Kneeling over him—blood, so much blood, dripping down his chin, was my husband. My Cyrus.

He looked back at me with wide, startled and terrified eyes. Eyes that were glowing red. Eyes that were framed with sprouting, raised black veins.

"Sevan," he breathed, his voice cracking. He looked down at his hands, also covered in blood. And then down at the man. As if startled to see him lying there, dying, Cyrus scrambled back away from him, backing into the wall. "Sevan, I…"

A little whimper-scream muffled over my lips as my eyes filled with tears and I backed across the room. "No," I muttered. "No, no, no." I shook my head, over and over as if it could make the last few minutes disappear. "You promised. You promised you would never let this happen again. You promised it would only happen once. You promised you would fix this!"

Cyrus knelt there, his breathing ragged, his eyes still that brilliant red, glowing so bright. Brighter than anything save the sun.

"I promise I have been fighting it, Sevan," he pleaded. "The burn..." He actually made a coughing-growling noise, sounding very much like a predator. "I swear I am burning alive. It calls... I can feel it, the only thing that will stop it is blood."

"These are *people*, Cyrus," I said, my voice a trembling whisper. "Real human beings. Just like me. Just like..." My lower lip trembled as I stared at the man I married. The man I didn't even recognize any longer. "Just like you used to be."

Cyrus tucked his knees up to his chest, making himself very small. "It wasn't...it wasn't supposed to be this way. It worked, I can feel, it worked. But this..." He stared down at his blood-covered hands. He just shook his head, at a loss for words. "I do not know how this is science. How this is magic."

I backed up, toward the door. To escape. "This is neither, Cyrus," I said quietly. "You went against the gods. And now you're cursed."

I turned. And I ran.

~

A SHARP GASP RIPS THROUGH MY THROAT, AS IF INDEED I have been running. The space around me is blurry. Dim gray covers everything. It all feels like smoke.

But it's all here, and I exist in two worlds.

The present.

Here in this room, at the House of Conrath. My brother

lying on the bed as science and magic once more changes a man.

But I'm also in the past, inside a body that has long since been buried in the ground.

I reach a hand out, trying to grasp…anything. To feel what is real.

All I feel is air.

And then dust chokes my lungs.

And I grip the smooth, firm surface of the fruit.

CHAPTER 16

I GLARED AT THE MAN AS HE PUT THE APPLE IN MY HAND, acting as if he were giving me gold.

He smiled. Though it was more of a sneer. A sidelong look, with the devil in his eye.

Kevork was an ugly man. He had a bulbous nose, turned red by too much wine. His skin was pitted and pocked. His hands were gnarled and his nails were always stained yellow, just like his teeth, the ones that were left, anyway.

"Come," he said, grabbing my arm and pulling me down the street.

It was lined with tents and merchants. Loud voices called, pitching food and spices, jewelry and shoes.

Dust billowed in the air. It was suffocating, especially in the heat of summer.

I loved the market. It was my favorite thing to do, to just wander and take in the sights and smells. Nothing was more alive than the market.

But today I was with Kevork. I'd rather be anywhere in the world than with the man I'd been promised to.

He greeted the man selling silk and cotton fabric. They laughed and joked and began talking money.

I stood there, not better valued than a fat sheep. Kevork held up fabrics to me, commenting on if the color would match my hair, bring out my eyes.

How it would cling to my figure.

How easy it would be to rip off come our wedding night.

Bile rose up my throat as I just had to stand there like a statue while these men laughed about young women on their wedding nights.

I was already an old bride. I'd fought my parents for the last few years, stalling them, telling them I refused to be pushed into a marriage.

But no more.

My parents had given my dowry to Kevork and told him we had to be married by the next moon cycle.

My fingers rolled into fists and my jaw tightened as my betrothed settled on some fabric for my wedding gown and paid for it.

I'd been born comfortable. Not the most wealthy in town, but certainly better off than the majority. But I hated it. Money brought arrogance and pride and the loss of humanity.

I was just a pawn my parents could use to further advantage themselves.

"Come," Kevork said, grabbing my arm and dragging me further down the street.

"Do not touch me," I hissed, keeping my voice quiet as I

jerked out of his hold. I looked around, making sure no other heard me.

Kevork chuckled and grabbed me once more. "It is my right, *geghets'ik*," he sneered, leaning in close. "I shall touch you as I like."

I jerked away from him again. "I am not your wife yet," I seethed. "And I will do everything in my power to keep your hands off of me even when I am."

His face hardened, his ugly face contorting with rage. "Watch your tongue woman," he growled. "Or I will have it for dinner."

I took a step away from him, walking backwards. "You can try."

Oh, he was going to kill me.

He lunged forward, faster than I expected his old age to permit. His wrinkled hands wrapped around my upper arms, crushing down hard enough I knew I'd be bruised later. Before I could even scream, he dragged me to the side, behind the tents.

With wide, terrified eyes, I realized we were in an empty alley.

I could see it in his eyes, exactly what he intended to do to me.

"No," I said, gritting my teeth. "Do not lay your hands, or any part of you on me."

"It is my right, *geghets'ik*," he said with a wicked grin.

I turned to run, but he grabbed me, shoving me against a wall. My head hit with a crack and little lights burst in my vision.

He flipped me around, and his disgusting hands greedily groped at my skirts.

"No," I muffled, still dazed. "Get…get off."

He hauled my skirts up and I heard the sound of buckles and fabric.

"No," I said again, blinking to clear my head.

I searched. My hands swept at the stone wall I was pressed against, looking for anything to fight back with.

"Step away from the woman!" a voice yelled.

My vision cleared, my thoughts less foggy.

A second later, Kevork was ripped away from me, just as I felt his warm skin pressing against private parts of me.

A possessed yell, scuffling.

I was frozen for just a moment as I realized just how close he'd been to being inside of me. Of how close he'd been from taking that one thing from me that I only had once to give.

So close, he was practically there.

Beneath me, I felt something sharp. My hands wrapped around it.

A piece of metal. Long and slender.

I turned, lifting its weight.

The two men were fighting, but all I could see was Kevork. I raised my weapon, and I brought it down through the air.

It easily found its way. Split his skin. Cracked bone. Pierced through tissue.

I embedded the rod through Kevork's chest.

He made a small gasping sound. His eyes swung over to me, wide, shocked.

And then he collapsed to the ground, further impaling the rod though his heart. He made one more gasping breath.

And then he was dead.

I was filled with horror. I was.

But I just stood there, stone faced, looking at his dead body.

"Are you…" a shaky voice asked. "Are you alright?"

I remembered that there was someone else in this alley, someone who had pulled the man off of me.

My eyes slid over, and met the most dazzling ones I'd ever seen. I get lost in those eyes. Green, dark green. Like the trees just before their leaves change color. Leaves in the forest at night.

He was medium height and build, but he looked strong. Lean arms and trunk. Hands that seemed powerful, powerful enough to stop Kevork.

His dark hair was thick and wild from the scuffle.

And his lips. The most beautiful lips I'd ever seen. The top one was slightly fuller than the bottom.

"Are you alright?" he repeated the question, his eyes full of fight and worry.

I nodded. I was still slightly numb, perhaps in shock that he'd very nearly raped me, and now he was at my feet, dead.

"Thank…" my voice came out rough. "Thank you."

"Did you know him?" the man asked.

I swallowed once, tasting blood. I realized I'd bitten my tongue at some point. I nodded. "My parents promised me to him."

I couldn't quite read his expression. I was still in too much shock.

"Did you love him?" he asked.

My stomach was actually ill at the suggestion. I shook my head.

The man nodded. He looked down at the man. "You tell them that he was robbed. That he tried to fight, but the robber killed him, and you escaped."

I could feel it, the numbness wearing off.

And surprisingly, it felt good.

I felt good.

I nodded. "What is your name?"

He met my eyes again. They were still difficult to read. "Cyrus," he said.

I took him in then. His ratty clothes suggested he was little more than a hard laborer. But he carried himself in a way that said he could handle himself. There was a humble confidence in the lift of his chin and the gaze in his eyes that I'd never seen before.

"Thank you, Cyrus," I offered. "I'm in your debt."

He shook his head. "It was only the right thing to do."

I shook my own head. "Most would not see it that way."

"A person is a person," he said. "No matter if they are a woman or a man."

I smiled, something fluttering in my stomach. No one had ever said such words to me.

"I'm Sevan," I said.

"Like the lake," he said, smiling.

I decide then that it was one of the most beautiful smiles I'd ever seen.

I nodded.

"It's very nice to meet you, Sevan," Cyrus said, bowing his head just slightly, but keeping his eyes fixed on me.

I smiled, feeling my cheeks warm.

CHAPTER 17

HESITANTLY, I WATCHED THE HUT FROM AROUND THE CORNER.
The streets were fairly quiet out here on this far side of town.
But I stood there, still. I hardly even dared breathe.

I saw him once last week. He spoke with a man,
engrossed in the conversation. And then the man stepped into
his shop, and dragged out a dead dog. Cyrus took it, and
carried it back to that hut.

Two days ago I happened to be walking down the same
road. And without looking up, I ran straight into a firm body.

It was him.

With smiles and hesitant words, we spoke.

He invited me to come see his work. He was studying to
be a physician.

But that dead dog... The nearly exiled location...

I hadn't found the courage just yet. So out here I stood.
Watching.

I rocked forward onto my toes. My body said *go*. My heart wasn't sure why he cared to say the things he'd said.

Go, every part of my body said.

I stepped forward. I crossed the street.

My heart was somewhere in my throat as hesitantly I called his name outside of the hut.

The fabric parted and there was Cyrus' face. "Sevan," he said in surprise.

I smiled, so nervous. "You invited me, so here I am."

"I was afraid you wouldn't come," he said as he stepped aside and let me in.

The space was dark. It smelled of blood and decay.

Slowly my vision adjusted, but instead of looking around, I looked at him.

I smiled hesitantly as he stood in front of me. I searched his eyes, and I was sure that it was genuine happiness to see me.

"I worried my work might scare you off."

I turned then, observing the small space.

That dead dog lay on a table. It was cut open, its organs set here and there. Beside it, there was also a piglet, cut open similarly.

In truth, his work did scare me a bit. Cyrus was studying to be a physician, but here were these animals, gutted. And physicians were men you only saw when you're at death's door.

"Come," he said, turning. He places a hand on my shoulder, ushering me in.

What I could not see before is now clear.

There was a mat on the floor, and on it, was a woman. Her skin was pale, damp. She looked so sick.

Beyond her, against the far wall, there was a table. On it lay a man.

He was dead. I knew it because his chest was cut open, and some of his insides were lying on the table beside him, instead of inside where they belong.

"Cyrus," I said in horror as I began turning, my stomach rolling. "I don't…"

"Please," he said, holding onto me. "The things I've learned today, I promise, they're fascinating. I will be able to help so many people now."

Warily, I looked up into his eyes. I wanted to run. To erase what I'd just seen from my memory. But there was so much excitement in his eyes, so much hope.

I couldn't deny him.

Hesitantly, I turned back, and he guided me over.

He explained, excitedly, knowledgeably, but I didn't understand. Something to do with breathing. Something about the air and the dust. I didn't really grasp what he tried to explain.

But Cyrus spoke with so much passion. The way his eyes lit up… The gestures he made with his hands. The excitement he declared at the possibility of helping so many people.

"It's amazing, Cyrus," I said, even if I didn't understand it.

He smiled, and it was so beautiful. "So many less will die because of this," he said. "If only people will give me a chance. People will live longer because of this."

There. It flickers into his eyes. A darkness.

"Who have you lost?" I asked, stepping slightly closer to him.

His eyes slid away from mine. A muscle in his jaw tightened. "My parents," he said. "They both died of illness four years ago. They left me alone."

I reached forward, but stopped myself before touching his arm. "I'm so sorry," I offered.

He looked down, to where my hand fell at my side once more. And as he reached forward, gently taking it himself, my heart fluttered.

"My days are generally filled with darkness and grief," he said. "But since that day I met you in the market, they have been a little brighter, Sevan."

My name.

Cyrus said it, and I felt it. It would never sound quite the same again.

"I haven't been able to stop thinking about you since that day," he said quietly. His eyes rose from our hands to my eyes.

I can't think of anything else, I thought to myself. But the words stayed trapped there, scared, in my mouth.

"May I see you again, Sevan?" he asked softly. "Soon?"

"Yes," I answered him in a breath.

~

I LAID THERE, MY EYES STARING AT THE CEILING. THE BED underneath me was soft, I was warm and comfortable, but I did not sleep. I counted the knots in the wood above my head. I listened to the sounds of my parents preparing for bed. For an hour after they lay down, I stayed still and quiet.

When they both breathed heavy and deep, I silently climbed out of the bed. Without making a sound, I crept to the door. I glanced back, seeing that they both still slept, and I slipped outside.

The air was still warm. The street was dimly lit by a half moon, and I navigated my way without any difficulty. Down the road. Turning at the grove of olive trees. And then toward the field.

A lone figure stood in the center of the field. His back was turned toward me, he stared off, toward the one lone tree that stood toward the back end of the field.

My heart fluttered as I watched him. A smile curled on my lips and I just stood there for a moment, observing him.

The line of his shoulders. The assurance in his stance. How intent he was, even when just looking over a field.

He looked over his shoulder then, and even through the moonlight; I could still see his eyes.

A smile pulled on my lips. One mirrored on his own face.

The wheat rustled around my dress as I stepped forward. Cyrus watched me the entire time as I came to him, his eyes never once left me.

"I'm glad you came," he said as I stopped in front of him.

I felt my face flush. But I didn't look away.

He took a step closer, lessening the distance between us. Gently, he reached out and took my hand. He just held it for a long moment, brushing his thumb over my knuckles, looking at it.

"It was difficult to get anything accomplished today," he confessed. "When all I could think about was you."

He looked up then, those eyes grabbing me. I saw such honesty in them. He's laid himself bare and open before me, for me to ravage him as I want.

"My grandmother spoke of love and obsession before she died," I said. "We don't know hardly anything about one another. But I…" I hesitated, because I wasn't sure how to put into words what I was feeling. "The way I feel when I think of you. How am I supposed to know the difference? How am I supposed to know what this is?"

He studied my face, and for the first time, I saw uncertainty there. "I don't know," he admitted. "The two don't feel very different right now. But I don't think it's the way it should be. I hardly know you, Sevan. But I feel this…pull. But I won't lie." He shook his head. "Obsession can feel a lot the same way."

A sad smile crossed my lips. I took a step away, holding his hand, in the direction of the tree. Slowly, I guided us on a walk.

"Then tell me," I said, "about your family. About where you came from, Cyrus."

In the moonlight, Cyrus looked infinite. He looked supernatural. Like something from a far away star.

He looked like someone who would change the rest of my life.

"I came from a family of star worshipers and mud healers," he said. And I tried to interpret his tone. There's a connection in his voice. This is his history, those were his family. But there's also doubt. Maybe a hint of shame. "We always lived on the outskirts of the city, where no one would throw rocks at us or curse our name." He looked out at the horizon. "Only a certain kind of people came to see my parents. Those who wished to know their fortune, to ask the stars what the future held for them. And those who did not believe a priest could heal them. Those that trusted the dirt of the earth and the herbs of the bush to heal them."

"Was it true?" I asked, my brows furrowed at the story. "Did they heal people? Did the stars speak to them?"

He shrugged. "Perhaps. But I also believe in the power of the mind. How many of those people only felt they were healed because they wanted to believe my parents had special abilities? How many *made* their fates come to pass because they thought it was written in the stars?" He shook his head. "I think there was a little bit of both."

Goosebumps flashed across my skin, causing all the little hairs on my arms to rise. It's incredible. Whether or not any of it was true, it's fascinating.

"I always wanted to become a physician, to study the human body," Cyrus continued. "But because of my family's reputation, no one would take me on as an apprentice. No one would take a chance on me that I was different from my parents. So I have been learning on my own. Studying, researching. It's slow. But despite my family, I will become a physician."

"You said they died four years ago," I recall.

His eyes cast about, not truly searching for anything. "They both grew ill just as I came of age. They worked and worked on one another. But all the mud in the world, all the herbs they could drink, did not stop whatever ravaged their bodies from within."

He takes a deep breath, and I can see the conflict he feels about his family. "I buried them behind our home. And I never looked at the stars the same again. I never trusted the earth again."

I looked over at him, seeing the pain and betrayal in his face. "But what if some of it was true, Cyrus? Surely it wasn't all for show?"

He met my gaze. "None of it is quantitative, Sevan. None of it can be proven."

I sighed, but my eyes rose to the stars. "I don't know. I suppose I've always believed that there is so much more in this world than we will ever understand. I don't believe anything is black and white, or that there is only one side to anything. But I do believe there are lines. Lines that must not be crossed."

"And how do we know when we have arrived at those lines?" Cyrus asked.

We reached the tree, and underneath the huge boughs, we stopped.

I looked into Cyrus' face. He searched mine, begging for the answer to his question.

"I think that is when we have to rely on our own instinct," I said. I took half a step closer toward him. "That is when we have to know right from wrong. I think there's something inside each of us that whispers that truth."

My heart jumped into my throat as Cyrus raised his other hand and brushed his thumb over my cheek. "Mine tells me this, Sevan. That you are inherently good. That you are meant for a life that is so much more than the one fate put you into."

I stared up at him.

"That's interesting," I said quietly. "Because from the moment I looked at you, I knew the same to be true for you."

Cyrus leaned in slightly closer, his palm resting against my jaw, his fingertips touching my hair. "I do not know if it is love or obsession, Sevan," he said. "But I do know that the thought of not seeing you tomorrow, or the day after that, or the one after that makes me feel tight and exhausted."

I leaned in slightly closer and nodded.

"I want to speak to your parents, Sevan," he breathed, only a small amount of space between our lips. "I want to ask their permission to officially court you."

My chest tightened and my heart flew with the sparrows.

I nodded again.

And slowly, as if our hearts had orchestrated it before, we each leaned in.

And as our lips met for the first time, I knew this was it. This was the one place my heart would always belong.

CHAPTER 18

I WATCHED IN HORROR AS, WITH DEFEATED EYES, CYRUS walked out the door.

Fracturing, my heart surged and broke.

"No," I breathed, shaking my head. "No. You cannot just tell me that I cannot be with the man I want!"

"Stop acting like a child, Sevan," my father dismissed me. He had already returned to the scroll in front of him as if this was only a conversation about the wind outside. "You understand how these things work."

"Cyrus is a good man," I begged. "He works harder than anyone I've ever known. He is smart and driven and he is going to do wonderful things someday. He only needs to be given a chance!"

"Perhaps so!" my father bellowed. "But no one in this town is going to sully their reputation by making ties with the likes of him and that family! And it will be a cold day in hell before I give him permission to court my daughter."

Tears welled in my eyes as I turned to my mother.

"I am sorry, my dear," she said. "But we love you. And we cannot allow you to be with a man who can give you nothing. No future."

A tear slipped down my face, forced out by anger. I shook my head. "And what about love? Does it not matter that I love Cyrus?"

Their expressions were taken aback. They did not expect such a strong declaration.

Cyrus and I had been meeting in secret for weeks and weeks. But I had only introduced him to my family today.

Love.

Even though it had only been weeks, I knew it with everything in me.

I loved Cyrus.

"I never loved Kevork, and he certainly did not love me," I said, my voice hard. "But that does not matter to you. You would rather see me married to him, even if he tried to rape me, than see me with someone who cared enough to step in, someone who treats me as if I am treasure."

My father's expression showed hesitation. But no shock. No remorse.

"I am sorry, Sevan," he said, but I knew he was not apologizing about Kevork, or the fact that he would have raped me. "But the answer is no. You may not see that boy again."

I looked over at my mother. Her expression told me the same.

I shook my head. My fingers balled into fists.

Without another word, I bolted out the door.

People crowded the street outside. I darted into the

middle of the road, looking up and down it, scanning. My heart grew frantic, panicked as my mother called my name from the door.

"Don't do this, Sevan!" she yelled, sounding panicked. "Do not turn your back on this family and go after that boy!"

It was a threat.

I didn't know if she meant it or not.

But I didn't care.

Down the road, I spotted the dark hair, the strong, set shoulders.

I took off running, pushing my way through the bodies, shoving my way through. Tears spilled down my face, a sob cutting past my lips.

My eyes fixed on the back of his head, I pushed through the crowd.

"Cyrus!" I cried out when only a few people separated us.

He turned, his eyes red and glistening. His brows rose as his gaze locked on mine.

I collided into his chest, circling my arms around him, burying my face in the crook of his neck, sobbing.

"I don't care," I sobbed. "I don't care what they say. I don't care what they think about me. I'm tired of being treated like coin and traded for whatever they need. I won't let them send you away. I won't let them keep us apart."

Cyrus hands came to my back, clinging me to him hard.

I felt safe. Secured. Wanted.

Loved.

"I cannot let you throw away your life on me, Sevan," he said quietly. His voice trembled. I knew how difficult it was for him to say it. "I cannot give you anything but a life of shame and dirt."

I shook my head, my brows furrowed as I looked back up at him. "I don't care," I said, adamant. "About the status. About the dirt. All I want is a life where I feel valued. Where I mean more than an advantageous trade. All I want is a life with you, Cyrus."

The tears streamed down my face, but I'd never felt surer about any words spoken in my life.

Cyrus' eyes sobered as he looked at me. And I saw it there, reflected in his eyes: everything.

The doubt in himself at being able to give me a life.

But the feelings that had been there since the first day we met.

"I don't know that I will ever be enough for what you deserve, Sevan," he said quietly. "But I will spend every day of my life trying to prove myself worthy."

He brought both of his hands to my face, cupping it with such gentleness. And peace sank into every corner of my body. There were no words to describe the way I felt, and the rightness of the moment.

"I love you, Sevan," Cyrus said. "I know it with every bone in me."

And it didn't matter, and I knew in that moment that it would never matter, the fact that I would never be able to set foot in my home again. It just mattered what happened from this moment forward.

"And I love you, Cyrus."

WE STILL HAD SO MUCH TO LEARN ABOUT EACH OTHER. IT may have been only two moon cycles since we'd first met in that alley. It may have been under circumstances of duress and necessity.

But two days later, Cyrus and I stood beneath that tree at the edge of the field. Wearing a dress borrowed from a friend, with a simple crown of field daises around my head, I stood with Cyrus, my hands held in his.

We married on that beautiful, sunny day. Pledged to love one another for the rest of our days. To support and uphold each other. To take care of one another in sickness or health.

I smiled the world's happiest smile, even though there was no one present beside myself, Cyrus, and the authority.

It didn't matter, because I would get to spend the rest of my life with the man I loved.

Cyrus' eyes danced with wonder and love. He held my hands so firm, so tight. I knew he would uphold every promise he made. Together, we would make our own life.

Man and wife.

We were pronounced.

Beneath that tree, I kissed my husband, the happiest I had ever been in my entire life.

I SMILE, WARMTH FLOODING THROUGH MY CHEST. I CAN FEEL them, Cyrus' lips on mine. The strength of promises wash through me.

But a little voice echoes across the field.

"Logan?" it calls.

But it's so far away, I can't even hear it, only sense its presence at the back of my brain.

"Logan?"

A shake ripples through my body, but as I wrap my arms around my husband, I do not move.

"Logan?" it calls again.

But I only stare up into Cyrus' green eyes and whisper to him how much I love him.

CHAPTER 19

I STAYED OUT OF THE WAY, KEEPING MYSELF IN THE OTHER room as Cyrus worked with the poor girl with the oozing cut down her leg. But that didn't mean that I didn't peek inside every now and then.

Pride welled through me as I listened to Cyrus work.

Despite everything, here he was, doing good. Working wonders.

She couldn't pay him in anything more than a sack of grain and four eggs.

None of them ever could.

But he helped them in whatever way he was able.

Every night, after coming home from the fields, he would either continue his study, or help those who came to see him.

Some nights he dragged bodies home, taking them out back behind the house. Carefully, meticulously, he would examine their insides. He would press here and poke there. He took notes on scrolls.

Other nights, he would lead home a pig. And they served as both a meal and research.

Dogs.

Chickens.

A bat.

A wolf.

It was not just their anatomy he studied, but what gave them their particular strength, their advantage.

No one understood life like Cyrus did.

No one helped him. No one taught him. He did it all on his own.

He worked tirelessly, his curiosity like an insatiable hunger.

He would never confess it to me, but he did turn to his roots. I would see him rub his hands with dirt and offer up a silent prayer before working on someone who needed his help. I would see him look up to the stars before he cut a deceased vagrant open.

Cyrus was a believer in science and magic. Even if he would never admit it, even to himself.

He worked so tirelessly. Long days that began before the sun rose and only ended hours after it had set.

But every night, he would crawl into bed beside me. Every night he would hold me and whisper about his day, make sure mine had been wonderful. Each night he pulled me in close and whispered promises of a wonderful life.

Every night was ours.

Every night was filled with whispers of love and commitment.

We lived in a hovel on the outskirts of a new town. Alone, with no family and no friends.

But we were building a life. Together.

And it was all I needed.

~

ONE YEAR LATER, A BRAND NEW TOWN. SO FAR FROM WHERE we had begun, no one knew anything about the man named Cyrus or his wife who walked away from a life of comfort.

We began anew.

Cyrus had learned so much. Had helped so many people. He understood the human body. Could seem to predict ailments, would try things no one else would think of.

After only a few weeks in our new city, Cyrus proved himself. Within a few more weeks, everyone came to see him when they fell ill.

We bought a real home. We had a real bed.

Cyrus bought me beautiful dresses. He could afford new shoes for himself.

More and more people trusted Cyrus to help them get better. But there was also a hint of fear in their eyes, and they whispered the name *sorcerer*.

But no matter their fear and awe, as long as he helped them live.

I couldn't blame them for their whispers.

Cyrus' practices were, at times, peculiar.

He continued to study animals. With the money people were now willing to pay him, he purchased dead animals.

Not just cows or chickens or dogs.

Exotic things.

An eagle.

A tiger.

A leopard.

These creatures were imported to him from far countries. They arrived in varying states of decay. Some fresh, some so far decomposed when they arrived that I had to turn and empty my stomach outside Cyrus' shop.

But he studied them all. Memorized their organs. Extracted their teeth. Drew vial after vial of their blood.

"What is it you're looking for?" I asked him one night as I sat next to the fire in his shop.

Cyrus stood hunched over a dead cheetah, the most beautiful creature I'd ever seen. It had come all the way from a land called Africa. I'd never heard of it before.

"Hmm?" he said absentmindedly as he removed what I was fairly certain was the animal's heart.

"You've never expressed an interest in treating animals," I said, watching the black blood drip down his hands. "Why do you keep studying them? What is it you're looking for?"

Cyrus set the heart on the stone table. Placing his hands on either side of it, he looked up at me. There it was, as always: that intensity. Like he's searching for something, excited, exhilarated. But it's the hunt that spoke to him as well.

"They're all so different," he said. His eyes rose to the wall where there were several long shelves. They all held glass jars, each containing the blood or heart of a different kind of creature. "They all have their different strengths and abilities. I just want to understand…" he trailed off. His eyes were unfocused, as if searching for the words. "I just need to know more. I want to understand it all."

"All of what?" I asked.

His eyes came to mine, and in them, I saw such an excitement, such spark. "Life," he said breathily as a smile began growing on his face.

CHAPTER 20

I STOOD AT THE EDGE OF THE WELL, LOOKING AT MY reflection. My hands came to my stomach, and with tears rolling down my face, I held my hands to its flat surface.

Two years we had been married. Two years we had been with each other. Two years we had been a tiny family of just two.

I should have conceived long ago. I should have a baby in my arms now. I should be looking into the dark green eyes of my son or daughter.

But I was empty.

Another sob ripped from my throat. I turned away from the well. I couldn't stand to look at myself any longer. I couldn't stand the disappointment I felt for myself.

We had spoken very little about it. Cyrus always reassured me that when the time was right, it would happen. He was happy just to have this time with me, just the two of us.

He meant it. I know he did. He was happy with our life.

But an ache had long begun in me.

A hollowness.

I needed more.

But maybe it wasn't in the stars.

Maybe it was my punishment for turning my back on my family. I'd found so much happiness with Cyrus. Surely I couldn't get everything I wanted and have children as well.

I stepped into Cyrus' shop, ready to help with whatever he needed me to do. I needed to forget myself.

He was just seeing a patient out the door. He coughed quietly as the woman hobbled out. He waved to her with a smile and closed the door behind her.

He turned, and coughed again, three times.

"Cyrus," I said, my brows furrowing. I stepped forward when I saw the sheen of sweat on his brow, his upper lip. I placed a hand on the side of his face. "You're burning up."

He coughed again, bracing a hand on his workbench. "Just a minor illness," he said, trying to brush me off. "I'll be fine tomorrow."

My eyes narrowed and I moved my hand to the back of his neck. It was just as hot. "You started coughing last night," I say. "Stay here, let me make you some tea."

He coughed again as I walked to the fire to boil the water. "Thank you, my love."

～

TWO DAYS LATER, CYRUS COULD NOT RISE FROM OUR BED.

He was sweating profusely. His body trembled as if he

were freezing to death. He could not hold down any food or water.

Soon, he was delirious.

I'd watched Cyrus work for two years now. I had picked up on many of his simple practices. So I tried everything I'd seen him do.

But nothing broke the fever.

"Sevan," he called out in the night. I'd been getting more water to try and cool him down, but darted to his side instantly.

I dropped to my knees beside him, taking his hand into mine and holding it to my chest. Tears welled in my eyes. His breathing was so ragged and labored. "I'm here."

"Sevan," he said again, his words slurred. "I don't think..." he struggled to speak. "I think this might be the same illness that took my parents."

I shook my head. "No," I said as a few tears broke free. But I forced my voice to be even. "No, it isn't. They tried to cure it with magic and earth. You know what you're doing. You know the science. The fever will break come morning, and you're going to be fine."

It terrified me when his eyes cleared for just a little while and they focused, meeting my own. Weakly, he raised his hand to the side of my face, caressing it.

"I promised to take care of you for the rest of my life," he said, his voice so regretful. "I keep my promises, my love. But I don't know if the universe is going to cooperate."

I placed a hand over his, shaking my head. "You're going to be fine." My lower lip trembled as his breathing grew more ragged. "You're going to keep that promise. Because I love you too much for you to leave me here."

He seemed to gain a little more strength, just for a moment. "I love you, too," he breathed. "My forever heart."

His strength gave out, his arm dropping into my lap.

"Cyrus," I said as his eyes slid closed. They didn't open. "Cyrus," I cried.

His chest continued to rise and fall.

But his breathing sounded so terrible.

I clutched his hand to my chest, rocking back and forth, tears cascading down my face.

I offered up a prayer to whoever would hear me. Loud. Shrill. Terrified.

I begged for my husband's life.

FOR TWO DAYS, I THOUGHT HE WOULD DIE.

His breathing would stop.

His skin was so hot I could barely stand to touch him.

He never opened his eyes.

He never responded to me calling his name.

But finally, I touched his arm, and his skin did not burn.

Finally, the sweat diminished.

Finally, he gripped my hand.

Finally, he opened his eyes.

"My forever heart," he said as I gathered him into my arms, holding him to me as I wept tears of gratitude.

CHAPTER 21

I LOOKED OVER AT CYRUS AS HE CARVED HIS WAY THROUGH A man who had died two nights ago. The family had donated his body to Cyrus so that he might further study.

I noted the hard set to his lips.

I saw the steady firmness in his hands.

I saw the raw determination in every corner of him.

It had been one week since my husband had nearly died. A week since he stopped breathing for a few minutes. A week since I thought I was a widow.

Cyrus was alive.

But he'd been odd.

Quiet.

Reserved.

More focused and determined than ever to learn. To understand.

I had asked him, over and over, what was wrong. If something had happened while he was sick.

But he only told me that he needed to work. He was fine. He just wanted to focus.

Something was different.

A frantic knock on the door sounded just a second before two bodies barged inside, one of them carrying a small child. They frantically started shouting about their daughter, to please help her.

Cyrus told them to lay her on one of the tables and he immediately set to diagnosing what was wrong with her.

"I…" he shook his head after just a few minutes, looking back toward her parents. "Your daughter is dead."

The mother's face hardened. "But she is not gone," the woman insisted. "I can feel her. Fix her!"

Cyrus' face seemed uncertain. But he looked at that poor girl's parent's faces. And he saw their desperation.

Turning back to the girl, he dipped his fingers in a bowl of ash beside his table. He rubbed it over his hands.

He leaned down, listening to her chest. He pushed his hands into her stomach, feeling her organs. He placed his fingers to the side of her neck, feeling for the pulsing of her heart.

For several minutes, Cyrus searched her body. He closed his eyes as he ran his hands through the air over her.

I watched in fascination as he leaned over her. I watched him take in a breath. And he put his face to hers, his mouth covering hers, and breathed into her.

He then put one hand on her chest, the other on her stomach. And he pressed. Depressing her chest a bit. In a rhythm, the same as a heart would beat.

He breathed into her once more, before beating her heart for her once again.

For several minutes, he repeated the process. Breath. Beats.

And then a sound came to every ear. A small breath in.

With wide, surprised eyes, Cyrus watched her.

Rise and fall. Rise and fall, her chest went.

She breathed.

And a moment later, her eyes fluttered open.

"Father?" she called. Her voice was hoarse. "Mother?"

With sobs and cries of joy, they snatched her, holding her to their chests. "Thank you," the father said, his eyes full of wonder as he looked at Cyrus. "You...you brought her back."

"You snatched her from death," the mother said, gently reaching out and touching Cyrus arm.

His eyes still dazzled, Cyrus gave a little smile and a nod.

The family, still together because of Cyrus, walked out, carrying their child like the most precious cargo in the world.

His eyes were still wide when he turned to me.

I beamed at him, amazed. I held my arms out, hugging him to me. "That was incredible, Cyrus. You brought her back from death."

"She's alive," he breathed. "She...she was dead. And now she is alive."

∾

I FELT IT, THEN. THE SHIFT.

Cyrus had been fascinated with life since the day I met him.

But from that day forward, it changed.
All Cyrus could think about was cheating death.

CHAPTER 22

I LOST HIM THEN.

I lost my husband. The man I loved.

From then, over the next two years, all Cyrus cared about was science and magic and death. He scarcely even saw me, though I was always there.

And then, two years later, after dozens of tests, he came to me with a gleam in his eye.

"I've done it," he said.

"Done what?" I asked. Fear started creeping into my voice. Because that look in his eye? It could lead to no good.

"Created the cure," he says. He held up a vial filled with black liquid.

"Cure?" I asked in a breath.

"The cure for death."

CHAPTER 23

"PLEASE DON'T DO THIS," I BEGGED THAT NIGHT. CYRUS whirled around his shop, gathering things. Double-checking notes. In general, pacing. "You have no idea what is going to happen if you take that! What if...what if it kills you instead?"

"I've run dozens of tests," he responded, though he was hardly aware of me at all. "I've made adjustments as needed. Every subject has been successful. This is going to change the world, Sevan!"

I grabbed his arm, making him look at me. His eyes were too bright. Too wild.

"Men are not supposed to live forever," I said, turning my voice calm. "It is the natural order of things, to one day pass away. You've done incredible things with your life, Cyrus. Is it truly not enough?"

His eyes narrowed. "There is so much more to this world. I will never have the time to learn it all. I will never live to see it all, and all the life it holds. This…" he held up the vial again. "This is *true* greatness. This will change the course of history."

Tears welled in my eyes. Slowly, my fingers fell away from him as Cyrus stepped out of my grasp.

He stood by the door. I watched as he unstopped the vial.

And tears rolled down my face as he brought the glass to his lips, and drank his creation.

~

"Is it a coma?" a very far away voice calls through the dark.

"She is still reactive," another one says. "This is something different."

"Is she ever going to wake up?" a familiar one asks with fear.

"I don't know," someone else says quietly.

My eyes flutter. Fuzzy shapes float above me. Hazy shadows mix with light.

"Logan?" someone calls me.

But I can't answer.

Not when my heart is broken.

Not when I've lost the man I love.

Not when terror is racing through my blood as I watch the man I married bound down the street like an animal. He leaps through the air. His eyes glow brilliant red.

Fangs extend.

He lands on top of the man.

And he bites into his neck.

Numbly, I sat in a chair, staring at the wall.

I could feel him, as if there were a tether tied between us. Across the room. Watching me. Waiting for a response.

"Please say something, Sevan," Cyrus said.

My eyes remained fixed on the wall.

Twice now he had promised me he would not kill again. Twice he had sworn he would find a way to fix this.

He had tried. I would give him that. Cyrus had spent hours in his shop, working and scheming and testing.

But three times now he had killed an innocent.

Three times now he had hunted down a person. He had grown fangs. His eyes had ignited brilliant, blood red. He had drunk their blood. Every bit of it until they were stone white, their body looking depleted and empty.

"I don't know if I can cure this," Cyrus had just admitted. "I don't know if I can reverse it. Any of it."

Something cold and heavy settled through my body at his words.

"And I don't know if I want to," he had said after. "The bloodlust," he had shaken his head. "I never expected it. It's...a terrible consequence. But Sevan," his voice had gone breathy. "This strength, the power in me. My vision. My instincts." He had taken my hand and stared up at me, even if I wouldn't look at him in return. "It may have only been seven days, but I can feel it, Sevan. The cure for death was successful. I will never die."

My eyes slid closed.

I felt sick.

So sick.

"Can you not be proud of me, my forever heart?" he whispered. His tone... I could hear his agony. His desire.

I couldn't find any words.

He had sat at my side for a long moment, just watching me.

He gathered my hand into his, holding it to his chest.

He was no longer human, but still, I felt his heart beating in his chest.

"Do you still love me, Sevan?" he asked in a terrified breath.

Still, words did not come to me.

So I had sat there.

Cyrus eventually let go of me. He sat across the room. He watched me.

And I could not find the words to answer him.

I COULD NOT TELL MY HUSBAND THAT I LOVED HIM.

But as disgusted as I was by what he had become, I could not bring myself to leave him.

I kept myself removed for those first few weeks.

But eventually, I found myself looking into his dark eyes. Eventually, I let him wrap his arms around me once more.

Eventually I let him whisper familiar words in my ear.

Eventually I let him back into our bed.

"Join me, my forever heart," Cyrus eventually dared whisper one night. "I cannot stand the thought of moving on in this life without you when one day the course of your life runs out."

I rolled over, my brows furrowing as I looked up at him.

"I created two doses," he said, placing a hand on my cheek. He softly brushed his thumb over my skin. "Join me, Sevan. Let us lead this new life together."

I reached up, gently touching his face. My insides twisted, filled with so much uncertainty. So much anger. So much doubt. And fear.

"And go through the bloodlust?" I said. "The inability to control myself? The loss of myself as a human?" I shook my head. "Cyrus, this is a path you set yourself upon. It is one I cannot join you in."

His eyes darkened. They filled with sadness and anger and betrayal. "Sevan, when I said that I would love you for the rest of my days, I meant it with every single fiber of my being. Those days never, ever have to end."

I still had my doubts. It had not been long. It would be years until we were certain.

I shook my head again. "I cannot."

CYRUS CONTINUED TO HUNT PEOPLE. HE DRANK THEIR blood. His fangs would lengthen and his eyes would glow, and he would drain them of their blood.

He continued to study.

But he could no longer practice. He could not control himself when someone walked in with a bleeding wound.

He adopted a new practice, though. That of exacting

control over himself. He was determined to not let the blood-lust take hold of him, turning him into a monster.

He hid what he was from our town.

And every night, wrapped in his arms, with my heart trembling and splitting in two, I stayed with my husband.

Every night, he tried to persuade me.

A lifetime of immortal strength together.

Endless time to see the world. To learn everything about everything.

A lifetime of he and I.

He swore he would give me the world.

But I would raise a hand to my neck. I would imagine how those people must have felt as he hunted them down. The terror that must have consumed them as they realized they were going to die at the hands of Cyrus.

No, I told him. Over and over.

His anger and hurt grew by the day.

He questioned my commitment I had made the day we married.

He questioned if I still loved him.

I could never answer him straight.

Because I wasn't so sure.

Screams.

Fights.

Bitterness.

I couldn't leave.

But I couldn't go where he felt destined to go. Into this new life.

I felt sick.

Every morning. Every night.

AND THEN ONE NIGHT, I WOKE IN THE DEAD OF DARK TO A liquid slipping down my throat. And Cyrus' hands clamped down over my mouth and nose.

Forcing me to swallow.

Forcing me into this immortal life with him.

CHAPTER 24

"No," I sobbed. "No, no, no, no, no!"

Tears rolled down my face as I felt the strength rip through me. I trembled as my vision pulsed and flashed, and every single detail around us became crystal clear. I could see…everything in the dark.

"No," I whispered as they swept through the dark.

They found Cyrus.

"Sevan," he breathed.

His eyes were wide. Terrified. He looked like he would be sick.

"No," I cried again. I shook my head. Horror filled me, made bile come up my throat.

I knew it. He had turned me.

In the end it hadn't mattered that I had told him no. Cyrus turned me, anyway.

"Sevan," Cyrus said as tears slipped down his face and slowly, he stepped toward me. "I'm so sorry. I only wanted to be together."

"No," I cried again. I took a step back from him as the fire ignited in my throat.

"I'm so sorry, Sevan," he cried as his face crumpled.

∼

I COULDN'T CONTROL IT.

The thirst was so all-consuming. It was all I could think about. The burning in my throat. The heat that would spread down to my chest. Out to my fingers. Race down my legs. To my toes. It consumed my brain.

Drink. *Drink.*

It was all I could focus on.

Within the first week of being cured of death, I killed seven people.

We could no longer go out in the daylight. It made hunting easier. Very few were out in the dark. But it meant no witnesses to our nightly activity.

Until the day a mother saw us take her teenage daughter.

She screamed for the entire town to hear.

With panic, Cyrus took my hand. We ran. So fast no one could see us. We ran, and we went home, and we packed.

We set off with our precious belongings and all the coin we had accumulated.

But it was not long in the next town before the same happened.

Out in the woods, a blanket thrown over our heads to keep the dewy rain off of us, I laid on my back.

"We will figure this out, Sevan," Cyrus assured me

through the dark that was so comforting. "I promise I will find a way for us."

When I had opened my glowing eyes for the first time, I was filled with utter hatred.

Cyrus had betrayed me in the darkest way.

He had taken away my choice.

My wishes.

He had forced this life on me.

But I was so delirious with the thirst. I was so consumed.

I needed him. I had to rely on his experience.

Together.

We were in this together, even if I hated him.

He'd spent every day of my new life apologizing. Being so attentive. Sobbing and asking for my forgiveness.

I couldn't give it.

"You've been better since you changed," Cyrus said in the dark. "I was getting worried. You were so ill. It seems the cure not only alludes death, but other illnesses."

I wasn't really hearing his words.

Absentmindedly, I placed my hands on my stomach.

I'd thought that perhaps my body had just been swollen with all the blood I had drunk.

But there, deep inside, I felt a flutter.

Just a small movement.

But distinct.

A sharp breath pulled into my throat. Emotion bit at the back of my eyes and they instantly welled.

"What is it?" Cyrus said, sitting up, looking around, on high alert.

Gently, I ran my hands over my stomach.

And instantly I knew.

"Cyrus," I breathed. My eyes shifted over to his, meeting them in the dark. I shook my head. "I was not ill all those weeks. It wasn't just stress."

His eyes flicked to my hands on my stomach.

I watched his expression change. It went slack, his eyes widening. His mouth opened.

Gently, he reached over, placing his hand on my stomach. "A child?" he said breathily.

I sat up, climbing to my knees. I placed my hand over Cyrus', holding them gently.

And suddenly, in that moment, it didn't matter anymore.

What he had done. That it was so wrong.

Here, inside of me, we were making a new beginning. A new future.

From that moment forward, this was what mattered.

Our little family.

"We're going to have a family, Cyrus," I breathed. And for the first time in so long, happiness rushed through me. I smiled. A breathy laugh came through my lips. "We… we're going to have a family."

Tears filled Cyrus eyes. But joy, real joy spread on his face.

It was a mirrored motion as we each reached for one another. We both held on tightly in an embrace. And in the moment, everything was right once more.

There in my husband's arms, I felt it again.

How much I loved him.

How I'd walked away from everything to start this life with him.

It had taken a turn for the dark.

But here we were.

Together.

W E LIVED LIKE ANIMALS FOR MONTHS.

The woods were our protection. Out in the wild the scent of human blood did not drift our way. There was little temptation. We separated ourselves. We built a hut to protect ourselves, somewhere to get away from the sun that burned our eyes.

When the burn became too much to handle, we took the day journey to the closest village.

Slowly, we began to learn control.

We could drink without taking it all.

We took only what we needed to survive.

But that meant leaving survivors. That meant witnesses.

So eventually, deeper and deeper into the forests we moved.

My belly grew. I could feel the tiny life growing within me. During the day as we hid from the sun, Cyrus would place his hand on my stomach. Quietly he would talk to the baby. We'd smile and laugh and plan for our future.

We knew we needed to get away. We needed to escape the country we had been born in and travel to somewhere far and remote.

But I was large with pregnancy. Even with my new abilities, my enhanced body, it felt dangerous and difficult.

"Cyrus," I said one night. I reached over, searching for the warmth of him in the bed. "I need to feed."

I rolled over, a difficult task. My belly was huge. The baby constantly squirmed, kicking against my insides.

It had to come any day now.

"Come, then," Cyrus said. He helped me to my feet, and hand in hand, we stepped outside our hovel. Through the dark of the fall night, we stepped over branches and leaves.

"We're going to need a name for the child," I said as I walked beside my husband. His hand tightened around mine, steadying me, even though I had no trouble. "Have you thought about what we should call him or her?"

Cyrus looked over at me, and my heart swelled just a little.

A part of me would always hate Cyrus for what he did.

But I also knew he hated himself for it. He regretted it every second.

I had to recognize that he'd done it out of love.

I'd chosen this man. And looking into his face right now, I'd choose him again, a million times over.

"I think I need to see him first to know his name," Cyrus said, giving my hand a squeeze.

"And what if it's a daughter?" I teased him.

"Then I shall be the luckiest man in the world," he said as he leaned in and pressed a kiss to my temple.

A sound in the woods whipped both of our heads back forward. Instantly, we both dropped into a crouch.

Flames flickered into view a long way ahead.

Voices floated to our ears.

Monsters. Demons. Soul eaters.

The words pierced through the night.

"Cyrus," I whispered. "They're coming for us."

I'd spoken so quietly, but suddenly, the mob went quiet.

And then a bellow, and the sound of pounding feet tromping through the trees.

"Run!" Cyrus yelled. Instantly, his hand wrapped around mine, and through the dark, we ran once again.

CHAPTER 25

I PRESSED A HAND OVER MY MOUTH, STIFLING THE SCREAM. I stalled in the middle of the road, hunched over in pain. My stomach contracted, all of my insides screaming under the pressure.

"Just a few more steps, my love," Cyrus promised, looking up and down the street in panic and fear. "Come, we just have to get inside."

We'd run for our lives. For hours we'd dashed through the woods.

The contractions had started. Only one every so often.

But long before the scent of humans hinted in the air they took control of me, coming every few minutes.

Finally, there was a town. Small homes and the village opened up.

I could barely move as we dashed through the streets, searching, looking for anywhere safe.

Cyrus aimed us for a seamstress shop, dark and empty.

I couldn't even stand straight as the contractions came after me, one on top of the other. Cyrus scooped me into his arms, carrying me to the door, and breaking the wood as he shoved it open.

A cry finally ripped from my lips as the pain grew to be too much. Cyrus laid me on the floor, among a pile of fabrics. He closed the door, pressing some of the strips into the cracks to seal in the noise.

I swore I was going to die. The baby was going to die.

Surely neither of us could survive so much pain.

"The head is crowning," Cyrus said as he pulled up my dress and looked.

I reached out, gripping his hand hard. And I told myself that everything was going to be okay.

We were here, together.

Cyrus was the father.

And he had helped women deliver babies before.

"It's time to push now, Sevan," he said. And I knew this time was different, because there was fear in his eyes.

But I just screamed, gritting my teeth together.

And I pushed.

I pushed.

I squeezed my husband's hand with everything I had.

And I pushed.

In a sudden rush of relief, the baby was out, sliding into Cyrus' arms.

So happy. Cyrus' face was so happy. He let out a startled, happy little laugh as he wrapped the child in the cloth that surrounded us.

"A boy," he said with the world's biggest smile. "It's a boy."

I smiled and I cried. Cyrus crawled up to my side, gently placing our son in my arms.

Little pink cheeks and little pink hands. Perfect lips and tiny toes.

"He's beautiful," I breathed pressing my lips into the wet mess of his dark hair.

Cyrus cried. Happy tears. He wrapped his arms around the both of us, pressing his lips into my hair.

"I love you so much, Sevan," he said quietly.

"Family," I breathed, rocking all of us gently.

We were a family.

CHAPTER 26

WE FLED. WITH A NEWBORN SON, NO POSSESSIONS whatsoever, and nothing at all to our names, we fled.

Across the country. We took a boat for several days. We stole a wagon and a horse.

They were very long days and nights.

Our son grew ill and recovered. We had no choice but to steal the food we needed. We snuck into places to escape the light of day.

We were much more diligent in being careful when we needed to feed.

But we never felt safe. So we kept moving.

But winter arrived, and with no home, surely our son would die.

He cried. He'd been crying for hours and neither of us could provide the warmth to warm him enough.

We crested the small hill, and before us stretched a lake.

Partially frozen over, but glittering and beautiful in the sunlight.

Beyond it, the shape of a village rose. But it was dark. Crumbled. Piles of rubble and ash.

And there, rising high above the abandoned village, great stone spires rose from the side of the mountain.

It was silent. So quiet. So still.

"There," Cyrus said, pointing to the long forgotten castle. "We will go there."

With a shiver, I tucked our son more tightly into my cloak, and we stepped forward.

I felt it then.

Peace. A sense of safety.

Home.

I felt it.

We were finally home.

~

WE WERE HAPPY.

Me. Cyrus. Our son.

In the beginning, it was so much work. The castle had half been burned from the inside out. In some places, all that remained were the stone walls. But we lived in the parts that were still intact. We built fires. We created a kitchen, though I very nearly starved us over the years with my inability to cook. We had our bedroom. Our son had his own room.

I came to forgive Cyrus for what he had done. In the end, I would always hate what he had done to the both of us. But he was still the same man who loved me more than anything. He was still the same man with the charming smile. Still the same man who worked harder than anyone I'd known. Still the same man with the incredible drive to become something great.

Roter Himmel. It's what we named our utopia. Our home. It may have only been the three of us, but we were happy in our Red Heaven.

A family of two vampires and a human son.

He never seemed to crave blood. He ate a normal diet. He played and ran around and was too loud and energetic. Just like any other boy.

He was human.

He grew.

For years we were happy. We were almost normal.

But our son… In the beginning we tried to ignore it, pretend it would go away. But his behavior was strange. And grew more concerning as he grew older.

The way he would crush his toys when he grew angry.

How he liked to play ruler over the army of pinecones he gathered as soldiers.

When he struck the poor cub he had taken in, killing it, when it grew impatient with his ceaseless teasing.

Cyrus and I looked at each other, concern in our eyes. We would sit down with him, talk to him about his behavior.

It should have been more alarming that he never showed remorse.

We thought we could love him into being good and kind. We thought we could teach him right from wrong.

Maybe we were just too distracted.

Cyrus returned to his studies. He continued to learn. He

gathered every scroll and tablet he could. On history. On war. On politics.

His desire for new knowledge did not ebb, but Cyrus had learned his lesson.

Our curse taught him where the line was to be drawn.

"Do you believe it, now?" Cyrus said one night as he crawled into bed beside me. Our son had just gone to sleep, now seven years old. "Do you feel it? The time slipping past us, as if we were invisible?"

I had to confess: it was obvious now.

Whenever I saw my reflection, I knew I had not aged since that night Cyrus turned me. "I feel it," I say. "We haven't changed. But what if…" I trailed off for a moment, gathering my thoughts. "What if we just aren't physically ageing? What if our time just suddenly runs out, and we die of old age, looking like we do now?"

Cyrus shook his head. "I feel it though. The sense of perfection. I feel incredible. This… I created this to be the cure for death. I know it worked."

I rolled toward him, pulling myself into his chest. I breathed him in.

I knew it, too. I didn't want to accept it, but I could feel it.

Cyrus had done it. He had beaten death.

CHAPTER 27

"I DO NOT CARE ABOUT THE CONSEQUENCES OF THE BLOOD lust!" our son bellowed. "The world needs to see what kind of potential exists, and the two of you have done nothing with it but hide in these mountains for eighteen years!"

My teeth clenched, my fingers rolling into a fist.

It was the same argument, nearly weekly, for the past six months.

Our son was smart. Brilliant.

He had his father's curiosity. He read everything Cyrus had ever studied. He understood the world, even if he had never seen any of it. Even if he had never had any kind of interaction with the outside world.

"You do not know what they will do to us when we step out into the light," Cyrus argued with him. "You did not have to endure those months of being chased with pitchforks and torches!"

Our son shook his head, his face hard. "They were the

ones who should have been running. You could easily have shown them what you were capable of. Had you the gall, you could have turned on those people and made them bend to your every whim."

I breathed his name, horror and disgust in my voice. "People are people," I said. "History is full of evil rulers and tyrants. Your father made a mistake. This was never meant to be used to dominate others."

He looked so disappointed.

It broke my heart.

Somehow, somewhere in the eighteen years of his life, I had failed my son.

"Create more of us at least," he said, looking desperately. "Give me the cure. Bring others into the fold. You forced me to live a life of isolation, but it does not have to be this way. You're strong on your own, imagine if there were hundreds of you! Thousands!"

"I will never do this to another!" Cyrus bellowed, stalking forward, getting in his face. Our son took a step back, hesitance in his eyes as he pushed his father to his breaking point. "You do not understand the curse we live with daily! You see only through the eyes of arrogance and power!"

With a look of disgust, he turned and walked away from the two of us. He stepped outside into the blizzard raging in the light of day, and the door swung heavily closed behind him.

"I am afraid of our own son," I confessed as once again, we were cast in darkness. "The darkness in his mind..." I shook my head.

Cyrus crossed to me, taking me into his arms and holding me tight.

He didn't say a word.

Because we both knew.

Something was not right with our son.

"WHERE WOULD HE GO?" CYRUS SAID AS WE TRUDGED through the snow. "He knows no one. There isn't another town for hundreds of miles. I'm sure he's just taking some time to cool off."

I shook my head, pushing through the snow that came nearly up to my knees. "Something isn't right, Cyrus," I said. "I just...I can feel it."

We went to his favorite places, one by one, searching for him.

He had not returned to the castle come nightfall.

He never stayed out in the dark, not in the winter.

Not with the wolves and the below-freezing temperatures.

He was not at the stable. He was not in the hunting perch. He was nowhere to be found in the frozen gardens.

The last place I could think to check was by the lake.

We walked and walked.

My toes were numb. I couldn't feel my fingers.

"I don't know why we are even doing this," Cyrus said, his voice hard. "The boy hasn't cared about us in years. He'd be better off to go on his own."

My stomach tightened and my heart gave a twist.

I didn't want to admit it, couldn't. It hurt too much.

But Cyrus was right.

He hated us.

But I couldn't just leave him.

"Mother," a very faint voice called.

Both of our heads whipped in that direction instantly, and in a blur we dashed toward the source of the sound.

Down at the water's edge, down a little cliff, we found him.

The ice was broken out on the lake, out twenty feet. A broken line led back to the shore. And there, lying on the rocks, sat our son.

His clothes were frozen to ice. His lips were blue, his skin pale.

Cyrus immediately scooped him into his arms and we dashed back to the castle.

"I fel..." his teeth chattered. "Fell in the water. I broke the...ice as I...came back to shore. But I couldn't...couldn't move once I got out."

"It's alright," I said through my tears. "It'll be alright."

I repeated the words over and over. Even when his eyes slid closed, and he did not open them again.

Cyrus carried him to our bedroom where a fire was raging in the fireplace. We laid him upon the warm stone floor and broke his frozen clothes off of him. I rubbed his skin, so frigidly cold.

For hours, Cyrus and I attempted to warm his body.

But he did not open his eyes.

His body never warmed.

And I heard it, as his heart beat its last beat.

Our son died right in front of us.

I COULDN'T STOP SOBBING.

My heart was broken, shattered into a million pieces.

Because I missed him. I couldn't imagine life going forward without his handsome face in it. I couldn't imagine not being able to put my hand on his cheek, I couldn't imagine not looking into his green eyes.

I couldn't imagine that this was all I would get, standing at the edge of his grave in the side court of the castle, knowing he was down there all alone.

But I also felt such a sense of relief.

No more fights.

No more fear.

No more wondering about the terror he might someday become.

It was over.

"We did our best, Sevan," Cyrus said quietly as he wrapped his arms around me as I stared down at the frozen, overturned earth.

More tears streamed down my face, freezing to my skin.

I'd never felt such self-loathing.

CHAPTER 28

A BOOM ECHOED THROUGHOUT THE CASTLE.

Cyrus and I looked up at one another from the study. Our eyes grew wide, instantly glowing red. We each grabbed for a weapon, two always within reach in every room.

With predator strength and speed, we darted through the many halls and stairs.

We froze as we stepped into the great entry hall.

The wood and iron doors lay on the ground in a splintered, shattered mess.

And waiting in the doorway, blood staining his chin, hands, and clothes, his eyes glowing brilliant red, was our son.

"Good evening Mother," he said with a wicked grin. "Father."

Horror filled me. My mouth could not close. My lungs could not take air in and out, and my tongue could not find words.

"It seems your curse did not end with the two of you," he said as he stepped inside, walking over the broken door. "Because just hours ago, I awoke inside a very cold and dark grave. And the burn..." He shook his head with a chuckle, his smile devilish. "You did not jest about the burn. But thanks to these incredible senses, it did not take long to find the nearest scent of a human and partake in my first meal."

I whispered his name then, the horror and terror in me washing through like a wave.

"It seems something truly remarkable happens when a vampire father impregnates a human mother," he said coyly as he continued walking toward us. "The unknown is if it can be replicated. If I am what I am because my mother was turned while carrying me, or if that is all it takes. An immortal father, and a fertile mother host."

"I beg you to end this line of thought here," Cyrus said gravely. "You do not know what you are toying with. You have no idea what curse you will bring upon yourself. Do not follow in my mistakes, son."

He laughed. "Son," he said mockingly. "Son means you love someone. Son means family, and would you not want your family to be together forever? If you loved me as your son, you would have wanted that for us, Father."

He shook his head, hatred filling every surface of his face. "You kept me alone my entire life, and told me that you were alright with me dying when the time came." He backed up a step. "Now is the time that I get the chance to correct your shortcomings and lies. I will find my own family. I will give them the promise of being together forever. And I will not suppress their potential."

I called his name again, my eyes pleading.

But I knew there were no words that would change his mind.

"We will meet again," he said.

It wasn't a promise.

It was a threat.

And without another glance back at either of us, our son turned, and left.

AS WE TRAVELED INTO THE SURROUNDING TOWNS OVER THE next few years, we heard rumors. Of a man from the mountains who took wives. Of a man who drank blood.

Whenever we asked where this man was, no one knew. Only that he traveled. That he visited far reaches of the world. And that he gathered wives by the dozens.

I felt sick.

I knew it was not the women that he cared about. It was the possibility of those children that might be conceived.

He hoped they would be like him.

"Cyrus, if he creates others like us..." I would shake my head, filled with terror. "There would be no stopping him. The damage he could do to villages. Entire towns."

"Countries," Cyrus corrected. His eyes were dark and stormy. "The world."

We had created a monster.

"We have to stop him," I breathed.

"We have no idea where he is," Cyrus said, his eyes

casting about the valley that spread before the castle. "He could be anywhere in the world at this point."

I stood at my husband's side, looking over our little piece of heaven.

"Then we need to prepare," I said. My heart started beating a little faster. "If it eventually comes to war, if that is the only way to stop him, we need to be prepared."

Cyrus looked over at me, and my gaze locked on his face.

"You already have the castle, my forever heart," I said, reaching for his hand. "Now you need a kingdom and an army."

CHAPTER 29

I LOOKED IN THE REFLECTION OF THE SILVER MIRROR ON the wall.

Blood dripped down my chin, splattering on the floor at my feet.

A woman lay there, as well. Dead. I had drunk every bit of her blood.

"Sevan," Cyrus' voice said from behind. But I did not turn to look at him. "Is something the matter? That is the third feeder you have drained in five days."

I looked down at her. And my heart shuttered a beat when I realized he was right.

"The burn," I said, shaking my head. "It won't stop. I can't make it stop."

He turned me, looking into my eyes. He searched me hard, as if he could read a diagnosis off my skin.

"Your Majes-"

The voice abruptly cut off as my handmaid stepped in and saw what was going on.

"Adeline," Cyrus said, looking over at her. "Find someone to help you take the body away."

She gave a little bow and quickly left the room.

It had been easier than it should have been. As people saw what we were capable of, we were either met with fear or awe. They either wanted to kill us, or worship us.

And we took care of them.

The people came.

We gave them a purpose.

We slowly built the town back up.

We had slowly built our own little kingdom over the past sixty years.

It was incredible what we had accomplished over these few years.

Incredible more that neither of us had aged a day.

When we should have aged out of our mortal lives years ago, we were both still going strong.

But no more.

"Something isn't right, Cyrus," I breathed hard. Already my throat burned hotter and all I could think about was more blood. More blood to ease the pain.

"Sevan," Cyrus said in utter terror.

But I couldn't hear his words.

All I could think about was finding another feeder.

I turned, and with glowing eyes and lengthening fangs, I darted through the castle, and leapt on the first person I came upon.

~

THE BURN WAS SO INTENSE, SO HOT.

But as I tried to rise up from my bed to go find yet another feeder, my strength was nowhere to be found.

"Cyrus," I hissed, my words rough and difficult. My vision was blurry as I searched around the room for him. My head was spinning.

"I'm here, my forever heart," he spoke softly.

I realized he had been sitting beside me the entire time. He took my hand, holding it close to his chest.

"This..." I struggled with the words. They came in and out with mountains of pain. My entire body was a burning inferno. Burning hotter than the sun. "This is the end."

Cyrus pressed his lips to the back of my hand, shaking his head. "No," he insisted. "I cured death. This is merely some illness we have yet to encounter. I can fix it. I only need some more time in the lab. I'll bring you with me."

Painfully I shook my head. "I can feel it, Cyrus. My time..." I winced, crying out as a new wave of heat scorched through me. "My time is out."

"Sevan," Cyrus cried. He gathered me into his lap, looking down at me. One of his tears slipped off of his face, splashing onto my cheek.

My eyes slid closed, too heavy to keep open.

"I hated that you took my choice from me," I said, the words coming out slow and heavy. "But our lives...what we've done...it is incredible. But if all of this were taken away," weakly, I waved a hand generally around. "I would still be grateful just that I could spend it all with you."

"Sevan," Cyrus cried again, holding me closer, pressing his lips to my forehead. "Eighty-nine years of immortality is not enough," he shook his head. "Nowhere near enough."

Another wave of pain shattered through me, but I didn't have the strength to fight it. It pulled me, down. Down to the dark. Down to where I saw an end to it.

But I needed one last breath.

With every ounce of strength I had left, I opened my eyes.

I met Cyrus' deep green ones.

I loved his eyes.

It was them that I first fell in love with.

Their intensity. Their determination.

"I love you, my forever heart," I breathed.

His last words muddled into the wave of pain.

I held onto it, letting it pull me down, down to where it ended.

And I was released into the darkness.

CHAPTER 30

A LIFETIME OF RELATIVE EASE AND PEACE IN A LAND FULL OF sand and jungles. A family removed from the others, a family looking for establishment and respect.

I lived an entire life among my brothers and sisters, my parents, and my grandfather, descended from a madman he called the Blood Father. I helped them grow an empire, discussed secrecy and safety for our kind.

And when my time came, when I reached the golden age of youth and maturity, they all hugged me one last time as a human and watched as I pierced my own heart with a blade and died my first death.

Eight others had done so before me.

Eight others had Resurrected from the dead after lying in the ground for four days.

On that forth day, I awoke, just as they said I would.

A vampire with strength and thirst.

But as the days turned into weeks, my dreams grew foreign. They turned to a land that looked so different, yet familiar. They showed me visions of a castle.

And a face.

And my heart felt sure it would die if I did not see it once more.

Cyrus, my brain one day screamed out as I sat up in my bed.

"Cyrus," I whispered the name.

His face floated before my eyes, so achingly familiar.

A poor man in an alley came rushing to me, one who saved a young woman destined to marry an unkind brute.

A wedding beneath a tree.

Nights of love and lust.

"Cyrus," I sobbed.

But my heart thundered in my chest. Elation filled my veins.

Sevan. I was Sevan.

I was also Jafari.

The family thought I had gone insane as I explained everything to them. They thought I was ill. Or that something had gone wrong in my Resurrection. I could not be the genesis queen. She had been dead for fifty-one years.

But how else could I know so many details about the legend of the man in a land far away? How could I know about the never-aging king amassing power across the world?

I had to get back.

I had to return to my home.

I had to get back to my husband.

Finally, an uncle agreed to make the journey with me. To cross the globe and find the land I could remember so clearly.

Spring turned into Summer and the leaves were just beginning to change when we rode through a mountain pass. The horses beneath us were growing weary, the journey had been so long and arduous.

But as we crested the pass and the land opened up before us, revealing a lake and a village and a castle, I smiled.

Home.

This was my home. *Roter Himmel.*

I spurred the horse on, and it broke out into a sprint, one last burst of energy. Its hooves raced over the grasses and rocks and terrain.

I'd swam in that lake at night under the light of the moon. I'd walked through these houses, now rebuilt and occupied, when they were burned to rubble. I'd walked this road up to the doors thousands of times and planted those fruit trees that now were large and fruitful.

I slowed the horse as we came up to the doors. Guards stood on either side of it, staring me down with dark eyes, ready to kill me if necessary.

Our home had changed so much since I was last here. So many more people. So much more glamor and activity.

But it was still the same.

The same feelings of peace and belonging raced through my blood.

The same sense of dread whipped me as I thought of the son we raised here, the one who was such a threat when he left.

I hesitated for a moment then, the pieces falling into place.

He'd been successful.

All the wives he'd taken, all the children he'd tried to create.

Malachi, my grandfather, talked of his father, the madman, the Blood Father, and creator. Malachi was every much a vampire, just like my son had woken to be.

As was my father.

As am I.

How many of us were there now?

There were my aunts and uncles.

There were my brother and sisters.

How many others?

"I need to see Cyrus," I said with a thick throat. I stood straight, tall. I stared the guards down.

It took an hour of arguing, but finally, they opened the doors and I was instructed to wait in the main entry hall.

I was angry. I knew every hall, every room, every passageway of this castle.

I wanted to storm straight to our bedroom and take Cyrus in my arms and never let him go.

But I waited.

It seemed an eternity before finally, I heard steps.

And my heart leapt into my throat as I saw his feet descending the stairs.

My view slowly grew, revealing strong legs. A lean middle. Familiar hands that worked magic and miracles. A powerful chest.

And then his face.

Cyrus.

Those lips I could never look away from. That proud nose. That wild, thick, dark hair.

And finally, those eyes.

The eyes I first fell in love with.

Dark. Deep.

But they were different.

They held a new darkness.

They held power.

They held anger and bitterness.

But I knew those eyes.

I'd stood frozen on the spot, just looking at him.

Tears pooled in my eyes and peace settled into every corner of me. A tiny smile fluttered to my face, even though he was looking at me with hardness and impatience.

"And who might you be that you think you may demand my presence?" he asked coldly.

I faltered, just for a second.

Cyrus had changed.

He'd begun building a kingdom before I died with Sevan's face. And now before me stood a cold king, and I didn't know what he was capable of.

But he was still my Cyrus.

Still my forever heart.

"It seems the magic of your cure had yet to reveal all its secrets," I breathed. It was all I could do to stay rooted in my place, to not go running to him, to not pull myself into his familiar embrace.

"If you think I know what you are talking about, you are

mistaken, woman," he said. But there was just a little bit of hesitance to his tone.

I found a small little smile on my lips. "You said eternity was what we were supposed to have," I said. "Perhaps we will still get it, just in broken intervals."

Cyrus' expression faltered then. His lips slackened just slightly and his eyes widened just a little.

"Do you remember how much of a mess this place was that first night?" I asked softly as I took one step forward. "Do you remember the owl's nest we had to remove from there?" I pointed to the corner of the hall, where an elegant table now sat. "Do you remember how cold it was?"

Tears pooled in Cyrus eyes, I saw them as I came close. His mouth fluttered, searching for words. He trembled.

I stopped just in front of him, looking up into his eyes with a new face.

"I don't understand how," I said quietly. "But I awoke across the world, and I remembered it all. It's me, *im yndmisht srtov.*"

"Sevan?" Cyrus breathed, his voice cracking.

I nodded, getting lost in those eyes.

And he buried me in his embrace, and once more, I was home.

~

"HER VITALS ARE STILL STABLE," A WATERY VOICE KNOCKS AT the back of my brain. "Her brain activity, however, is off the charts."

"And there's nothing you can do to wake her up?" another muffled sound floats across my thoughts.

"I'm afraid of the long-term damage I could do if I interfere with...whatever is going on inside that head of hers."

They sound so worried. So scared.

But I can't grasp it.

Not when I'm so relieved to be alive. To be with the man I love.

CHAPTER 31

MORE DESCENDANTS WERE DISCOVERED OVER THE YEARS that rolled into more than a century. More and more children and grandchildren and great-grandchildren were brought into the world.

Rumors spread of our son's amassing army. Talks of impending war rippled throughout Roter Himmel.

All we could do was prepare.

We built our kingdom. We amassed wealth. We bought armies in preparation.

And then, after 153 years together, I once more grew ill.

Once again, there was not enough blood in the world to sate my thirst.

And in another moment of agony and utter grief, Cyrus held me, as again, I died.

For 121 years I stayed dead, lost to the world.

And then for 19 years, I lived a tumultuous life as Helda, caught in the middle of a battle against the Blood Father trying to take over the world. My great-great grandfather, Dorian, influenced our family for the good, protecting the innocent lives the Blood Father wished to dominate. Protecting the secret of our kind.

And when the time came, I died my first death.

Four days later, I awoke as a vampire.

And six weeks after that, I remembered it all.

My previous life as Jafari.

My first life as Sevan.

Again, I returned to Roter Himmel.

Once more I had a bittersweet reunion with my Cyrus.

He waited for me. Between Sevan and Jafari he had never moved on, never sought out another. And for the 121 years I had been dead, he had held onto hope that I would awaken once more.

After all this time, Cyrus still held to his vows.

The world had changed much in the past century. Alliances had formed. All descendants had been accounted for.

The son Cyrus and I had created, the Blood Father, had created seven sons of his own, and twelve daughters.

Two of those sons and three daughters had allied with Cyrus, knew that we must keep our kind a secret if we did not wish to be eliminated by the rest of the world.

And then finally, word of our son's return was sent to Roter Himmel by messenger.

Our son was coming home.

And he was going to finally put an end to our stopping him from taking over the world.

THE WAR WAS NOT FOUGHT AND WON IN A FEW MERE WEEKS.

The mountains that surrounded Roter Himmel became the battlegrounds for a bloodbath that went on for seven years.

Countless lives were lost. Our home was very nearly destroyed. Famine was the threat that nearly caused us to lose. And as the humans died, there was little more for us, the vampires, to survive off of.

But then, on a crystal clear night at the beginning of spring, I paused in battle, turning across the field, as Cyrus and our son finally came face to face in battle.

With swords and fangs, they fought. It was like watching two lions, and the only outcome was death.

It was agony. I had to watch the two people I loved most in this world fight to the death. My husband that I had sacrificed everything for, and the son I had loved and carried and raised.

And everything in me froze, everyone on the battlefield seemed to turn to watch, as Cyrus knocked him to his knees.

I saw that look in Cyrus' eyes. The utter despair. The anger. The horror. The grief and regret.

It all flashed through his eyes, just as he brought the sword down, and cut off our son's head.

His body collapsed to the ground. His head rolled a little way down the hill. His blood stained the rocks and grass.

Tears rolled down my face.

Tears slid down Cyrus'.

It was over.

OUR GRANDSONS AND DAUGHTERS WHO HAD ALLIED themselves with our son were taken into custody and thrown into the dungeon. One grandson and three granddaughters had been killed at some point during the war.

And finally, after seven bloody years, and centuries before, it was over.

Except it wasn't.

Battles and insurrection continued for centuries. Times of peace and then times of rebellion.

But in the end, order was established.

With so many of us now, leadership was impossible to maintain from Roter Himmel. In a night of sleeplessness, Cyrus and I came up with the idea of the Houses. We trusted the descendants of Dorian and Malachi. They would help. We could train them, teach them how to be leaders, and then send them out into the world.

And so the age of order began.

I FEEL IT. THE RISE BACK TO CONSCIOUSNESS. I FEEL CLOSER to the light, closer to the present.

As if being sucked through a tunnel, I rocket through all of my lives.

First Sevan, and then Jafari. Helda, and then Shaku. Antoinette and Edith. And then I was born as La'ei.

And then Itsuko.

I searched for my life as her.

243

A village. A small village by the ocean. A simple life, but one as an outcast, shame on my mother for not knowing my father.

And then…and then darkness.

Screams and blood. Bad…bad everything.

Where was the rest?

Why couldn't I remember what happened after that Resurrection?

I scramble for it, groping through the dark.

Then the light and the warm call for me. I rise to the surface.

And I open my eyes.

CHAPTER 32

SOME KIND OF INSECT CHIRPS LOUDLY IN THE DARK. I SIT IN A wooden swing on the veranda at Alivia's House, Eshan curled in a ball next to me, his head in my lap. A soft breeze doesn't do much to cool the air down.

I'd woken up, totally alone in the room, except for Eshan, asleep in a chair in the corner. But as soon as I called his name, he'd sat up, and started yelling for Alivia and Nial.

I'd been in some kind of trance-like coma for two days. My eyes would open and close, but they never moved, only stared at nothing. I could move, but I seemed frozen in the bed.

They'd called for me, tried to wake me up, but I had just looked empty and lost.

Now I was fine.

Dr. Jarvis ran tests on me, checked me over from head to foot. He couldn't find anything wrong.

"I'm okay," I said, standing and pushing past everyone making a fuss. "I'm just starving right now."

They'd watched me as I ate like I'd never eat another meal. It was getting seriously annoying.

"I swear, I'm okay," I insisted around a mouthful of something so Southern I didn't have a name for it. "When you've lived a life as nine different people I think it's justifiable to have a couple of wacky days to get your head back together and remember."

Alivia sat down beside me. "Everything?" she asked.

I nodded. "All of it. The clearest is life as Sevan, but everything else is there. Except...except my last life before being Logan. There's something weird going on there."

I'd dismissed her then, saying I didn't need to talk about it, anymore.

So here, I've found myself back on the veranda with my little brother.

"How can you not be insane?" Eshan asks quietly. "You say you've been nine people, that you remember them all. Does that make you schizophrenic?"

I chuckle and brush a hand over his shoulder. "I felt like it before," I say. "My head just felt like a total mess with all these memories and voices thrown into this chaotic vortex. But, whatever happened over the last few days . . . " I paused, looking up. Lights dot the horizon. "It sorted my brain out. I'm still Logan. But a part of me is La'ei, and Antoinette, and Jafari. The biggest part is Sevan. But I'm still Logan."

Eshan sighs and shakes his head. "This whole thing is pretty nuts," he says. "That there's all this history and these politics and whatever, they all exist, and have been going on for thousands of years, and no one knows about it."

"I wish you'd stayed in the dark about it," I say.

Eshan shrugs. "You've kind of always been a bitter loner, Logan," he teases. "I'm guessing you need someone to talk about it with."

I smile. "Thanks, E."

He rolls over onto his back, his head on my thigh, and looks right up at me. "So what's the plan now? Are you really going to Austria like you told us all you were? Are you and Cyrus…going to be…husband and wife, or whatever?"

My eyes shifted to the horizon again.

I had to look deep. Dig down past my heart and into my core.

"Roter Himmel is my home," I say. "Cyrus, he's made a million bad decisions, done some bad things, but he's home."

Eshan doesn't look so sure about Cyrus. But a hopeful little look sparks in his eyes. "Can I come with? This place doesn't even sound real. A castle, and you, a queen?" He laughs.

"Yeah, right!" I tease him. "Mom and dad are going to kill you for running off like this. You're going straight home tomorrow."

And teasing and laughing, I get one last amazing day with my brother.

CHAPTER 33

I WALK INTO THE SHOWER AS THE SUN RISES THE NEXT morning. I strip down, tossing my clothes in the bin and step into the cool water.

No hot showers in this region, not this time of year.

As I wash my hair, I think back on this life. Particularly the last few weeks.

I understand now why Cyrus was so anxious for me to die when he first met me. I understand why he was so impatient.

When I told him that I needed some time to close out my life and we bargained for time, it was like a game to him. Cyrus loves his games.

It wasn't something that really came into play until my life as Antoinette, when Cyrus had already lived life as a vampire for over a thousand years.

I think back on all the little details of our time together in that house in Greendale. The looks he gave me over particular things. Over little things I said. When he took notes of little facts about my life, like how I believed in reincarnation, or the fact that I couldn't cook anything.

Those were all little signs and clues of Sevan.

But there were other details, too.

The way he held my hand at times. The way he played along with the part of Logan's boyfriend. The way he charmed my parents and Amelia. The way he saved me from Shylock.

Those details. Those were just about Logan.

And those final moments before I died the first death with this face, the guilt Cyrus admitted to.

My chest aches.

Cyrus has never loved another woman. His devotion and commitment to Sevan is astounding.

But there was that confession just before I died. *The guilt of feeling as if I am betraying my wife. Because when I look at you, Logan...* And I swear I can remember him pressing his lips to mine just as I died.

I'm ready.

I shut the water off in the shower and I step out.

I'm ready.

I'm going home.

I'm returning to Roter Himmel.

I can announce to the world that the Queen has been found again.

And I'm ready. For Cyrus.

For us.

With excitement, I get myself ready for the day. I dress, I do my hair, put on some makeup. I start packing my things.

I'm so ready.

I consider calling, or at least texting Cyrus, but I smile at the idea of walking up to the castle, as I've done so many times before, and surprising him.

I love the look on his face at our reunions.

He might know where I am, that the time is here, but he's been so understanding in giving me my time to sort through all of these emotions I've had to deal with.

I can't wait to see the look on his face again.

With my bag packed, I step out and follow the sound of voices.

Alivia, Rath, and Nial are all in the dining room talking. Each of them look up as I enter, waiting for whatever new levels of crazy I'm about to unleash on them.

"I'm going back to Roter Himmel," I announce. "Today. I'm going to fly with Eshan back home, smooth things over with our parents. And then I'm going back to Austria."

Alivia raises her eyebrows, her expression surprised. "So…so soon?"

I nod. "I needed time to straighten my head out and well, it was some power nap I took." I laugh at myself. I'm giddy, filled to the brim with anticipation. "And it's time. I've put Cyrus through enough in the past two weeks. I need to go home."

Rath stands, facing me. His expression is uncertain. Wary. "Logan, are you sure you're ready?"

I take a step forward, wrapping my arms around him. "I am," I say quietly. "Thank you. Thank you for coming here with me. And for keeping me safe for the past sixteen years.

I'm going home. I think it's time you get comfortable in yours again, too."

I let go of him, looking him in the eyes.

And like a weight lifted off of him, I swear I see the burden of protecting me lift out of his eyes.

"I have a favor to ask of you, Alivia," I say, looking over at her. "There's still one last piece of my identity I need to fit together."

She gives me a look of nervous anticipation, and I know she knows what I'm about to ask.

"I want you to come and identify my biological father," I say. "For my own curiosity, to know my other half. And for safety reasons. I've been in these politics for...for a really long time. And there are a million reasons why I need to know who he is."

Ian walks into the dining room then. His lips are set thin, his body tense.

I know what I'm asking.

For her to return to a place where she was held captive for a month, where she was tortured. And I'm asking her to go find a man she slept with once and then never saw again.

But, I'm asking.

"Of course," Alivia says, but her tone is tight. "Anything."

I smile, hoping she can see my appreciation.

So we prepare to leave.

I think I expected this visit to the House of Conrath to be longer. I kind of expected that eventually I'd get to know all of her House members and that at some point Ian and I would hash it out and eventually learn to deal with each other.

But I have such big things on my horizon.

This is just one House. And while it may be my mother's House, soon I will be involved with the affairs of all twenty-seven Houses. Soon I'll be dealing with Court again and the significance that my return will mean for our entire world.

Shit.

This is so big.

How the hell am I supposed to handle all of this?

You're not doing it all on your own, a voice from long ago whispers to me. A voice that is my own.

With our bags packed, everyone gathers in the entryway.

And to my surprise, Ian carries a bag for himself along with Alivia's.

"Not a chance in hell I'm letting her face Cyrus again alone," he says to me with a hard look in his eyes that dares me to tell him no.

"Fine by me," I say, holding my hands up.

"Good luck," Elle says as she crosses to me, pulling me into a hug. "I hope you find your happiness. Tell Cyrus hello for me."

"I will," I promise, hugging her tight. She backs away and I turn to Aster. "It was really nice to meet you, Aster. Maybe you and your mom could come visit me sometime and we'll get more time to get to know each other."

She smiles broadly, nodding.

All of Alivia's house members watch us, studying me. I offer them a little awkward smile, wondering what they're thinking.

But not really caring.

"Can we hope that with you back, that husband of yours

will be content to stay in Roter Himmel for a while?" Christian asks. And there, I see the darkness in his eyes, the darkness put there when Cyrus somehow killed, or was the cause of his father's death.

"Don't give us a reason to come back for a good long while, 'k?" I say with a wink.

He winks back.

"Are you sure you're alright?" Alivia fusses, speaking to Nial Jarvis. "This is so sudden. I feel like I'm just dumping everything on you and running."

"Things will be fine, Alivia," he reassures her. "It isn't as if we haven't dealt with the unexpected before."

She smiles, but it's forced.

In her eyes I can see the terror.

I wonder again: what did Cyrus really do to her?

But I have to force that thought down. The past is in the past and we can only learn and grow from it.

I turn to Rath. "And what about you?" I ask. "Where do you go from here?"

He steps forward, placing his hands on my shoulders.

"I've spent the last sixteen years watching over you, Logan," he says. "You've given me purpose, something to focus on. But this is your time," he says, his eyes gathering weight. "You have others around you. You have those in your service. But what I know is this: that you don't need anyone but you, my Queen."

He takes half a step back, and dips into a deep bow. And when he rises, there's determination. "It is time I return to my own home. It is time that I returned to the House of Conrath, where I belong."

I look over to Alivia. Her eyes are filled with tears and her lower lip trembles. Without a word, she crosses the space and wraps her arms around Rath. Neither says a word, but I feel it, the unspoken forgiveness that flows between the two of them.

"Thank you," I say, offering Rath a little smile as he looks over Alivia's shoulder at me. I turn my gaze to the rest of the House. "Thank you all for your hospitality. It was nice to meet you. Until we meet again, I suppose."

Looking over at Eshan who waits beside me, I turn, and we walk down the big, wide steps down to the cars that wait for us just outside the doors.

"You even talk different now," Eshan says.

"What do you mean?" I ask him, my brows furrowed.

He pins me with a look. "You talk all formal now. Older words. And you swear a lot less."

Holy shit, he's right...

I laugh, shaking my head and ruffle his hair.

Smith steps out of the house, immediately slipping into the driver's seat. He'll be bringing Cyrus' car back to this house once we all get on the plane.

The four of us load our bags into the trunk, and squishing in tight, we climb in.

The weight of what is coming distracts everyone into silence as we navigate to the nearest airport. It's a private field, one that accommodates the private jet Alivia arranged to take us back to Greendale and then across the globe to Austria.

We pull onto the tarmac, easily finding our waiting jet. Smith parks beside it and we all pile out, gathering our bags, which an attendant loads into the plane. With a quick goodbye to Alivia and Ian, Smith climbs back in the car, and takes it back to the House of Conrath.

"How am I just supposed to go back to normal tomorrow?" Eshan says as our bags are loaded. "Never mind how pissed mom and dad are going to be. I just spent four days as a vampire, learned my sister is a couple-thousand-year-old Queen, and that a seriously badass King is my brother-in-law. How the hell am I supposed to just go back to a normal life?"

Ian clamps a hand down on his shoulder. "You count yourself as damn lucky. You enjoy a drama-free life."

Alivia huffs a laugh, takes her husband's hand, and leads him into the belly of the plane.

"You'll be fine," I say, offering Eshan a reassuring smile. "And for what it's worth, I somehow doubt you're just done with all this craziness."

He smiles excitedly, and I wonder how much of this reality ever hit him. If he remembers that he killed someone. If he remembers what it felt like to drink a human's blood.

I hope he doesn't.

He scrambles into the jet, going off about how cool it is that Alivia has a private jet at her beckoned call.

I'm about to head in when my cell phone rings.

I pull it out to see Larkin's name.

"Any updates?" I ask without a greeting.

He lets out a breath. That slight moment of hesitation sets my blood cold. "I've caught the perpetrators," he says, his voice grim. "They're in custody."

"That's great," I say with relief. "I'm actually on my way back right now."

"There's something more, my Queen," he says solemnly. "I caught them leaving your parents' home."

And now all the blood has disappeared from my veins. My internal organs have turned to ash.

"There was a reason the attack on Cyrus was feeble," Larkin says. "I do not think it was him they were truly after." There's a long pause. And I feel the air grow heavier. "I think they were actually looking for you, Sevan. And now they're trying to draw you back."

"What do you mean?" I breathe.

One more pause, and I can't breathe anymore.

"They killed your parents."

And the world goes silent as a high-pitched ringing sets off in my ears.

CHAPTER 34

I THINK I BLACKED OUT MENTALLY.

One moment I was talking to Larkin on the phone.

The next a car was picking us up from the jet and the humidity was gone and the landscape was familiar. Security from the House of Valdez was swarming.

I blinked, looking around.

All the faces were solemn. Alivia. Ian. Eshan was totally stark white.

Did I tell them all? Did we talk about it? Do they know?

I snap into myself as we turn down our street. Everything comes crashing in as my childhood home comes into view. The red brick. The driveway where I used to draw pictures with chalk. The grass I started mowing when I was twelve.

I think they were actually looking for you, Sevan. And now they're trying to draw you back.

Darkness gathers in my chest as we park at the curb.

Black ink spreads through my veins. A thunderstorm rolls in through my brain.

I open the door and stalk across the grass. I shove the door open with enough force to crack the doorframe.

But my determination depletes as I see the blood.

A smear of it goes from the front door, through the living room, around the corner. Just past the corner, I see my father's wheelchair turned over.

"No," I breathe in horror.

I slowly step forward. Through the living room. I turn that corner.

So much blood.

It's smeared all over the kitchen. A bloody handprint is on the pantry door. Track marks from the wheelchair cut through streaks of red.

This was an animal.

They played with my parents.

They toyed with them like mice.

I turn when I hear sound.

"Eshan, no!" I yell, holding a hand out to stop him from seeing it all.

But his eyes are wide, looking around in horror.

"No, no," he says, his lips quivering. "Where are they? Where's mom and dad?"

I pull him into my chest, which is difficult considering he's inches taller than I am. "I will deal with this," I promise him. "I will make them pay."

From the basement, I hear Larkin call my name.

My eyes ignite and I feel my fangs lengthen. Ian and Alivia hesitantly step inside, taking in the carnage.

"Stay with them," I tell Eshan, pushing him toward Alivia.

I can feel the power ripple through me. The strength of the rhino. The speed of the cheetah, the stalking abilities of the jaguar. It flows through me, created by Cyrus so, so long ago.

I open the door leading down, and step onto that first stair.

I smell it.

Their fear.

It's intoxicating. My blood sings for theirs, to spill every drop of it, to see it wasted into the dirt.

I step off the stairs and turn into the dim light of the unfinished basement.

Larkin did me proud.

He holds them captive.

A huge stake is driven through each of their wrists, through their ankles, and one through their stomachs, nailing them to the wooden studs behind them. Blood is pooled on the ground beneath them, some dark and congealed, some fresh and wet.

But the moment I see their faces, I feel the fear and the past slammes into me with the force of an avalanche.

WAKING IN THE ABSOLUTE DARK WITH NEARLY NO AIR WAS terrifying.

Using the strength I didn't know why I had, to fight my way through the wooden box was terrifying.

Having a crushing force of dirt collapse in on my face

was terrifying.

Digging my way through that dirt was terrifying.

Climbing out of the ground and finding myself in the outcasts graveyard was bone chilling.

But the burn in my throat, the way my nostrils flared, smelling the air: that was instinct.

I knew where I was going. I knew the way back to the village and where everyone slept. But they didn't have names. They were only bodies with the solution to my burning.

I took one and I drank and I drank until the burning was only an ache in my throat.

But in horror, I understood.

I could never show my face again.

I had been dead, and now I wasn't. And now I had killed someone I had known my whole life.

My life as Itsuko was over.

For weeks I hid, keeping to the forest, trying to force myself to drink the blood of the animals I found, but it was never right. I found myself vomiting it back up, and always, I went back to the village at night, and killing someone I did not want to kill.

One night I had a dream. Of a man. A man with captivating eyes. A man with beautiful lips. A man with power in his hands and heart.

"Cyrus," I whispered as I woke up.

The next night, I went down to the docks and spoke to a captain, asking how I could get from this corner of the world to the land far away known as Austria.

He told me how much money he needed to take me to the

closest point he could.

I was to return in two nights.

It wasn't hard. I was silent and quick and no one even saw me. I snuck into homes and I stole what I needed.

And I wondered how I got here.

I was in the territory of the House of Himura. Considering I now remembered my life as Sevan, I knew I had to be a daughter of a Royal. As Itsuko, my mother did not know the name of my father, only that he was a wealthy man who had passed through our village and took her to bed.

And here I was.

My mother had no idea what my father was. Or what I would become one day.

And here I was, an unknown Royal. Here I was, Sevan and Itsuko.

I returned to the dock after two nights with the money. I boarded the ship. And we set sail for a long journey.

But when I woke after sleeping the second night, two men stood above me, wearing wicked smiles.

A man with a scar down the left side of his face, barely missing his eye. And a man missing one of his front teeth.

"Welcome back, Queen Sevan," one of them said with glee in his eyes.

The other grabbed me by the throat, picking me up and lifting me off of my feet. I kicked, tried to scream, but his Born strength held me immobile.

"We knew we would eventually find you, and finally we found you first," one said.

"What do you want?" I choked.

He pinned me against the wall, his hand closing tight.

"You are the key," he said, bringing his face close to mine. "The key to ending this whole monarchy. The key to ending the banishment."

My eyes widened.

There were thousands of Born in the world, those descended from the five exiled grandsons. The ones who had been banished from our lives.

"For all these years we have tried to take out Cyrus and his blood descendants at Court," the other hissed. "But never to any avail. They are too loyal. Too comfortable. Cyrus is too well guarded."

The man holding me grinned, leaning in a little closer.

"But the King has one weakness," he said softly. "One thing he will do anything for, give up any throne for."

My eyes widened and my heart stopped beating.

Me.

They were going to use me as the bargaining chip to tear down everything we had built. And I knew he would do it. To get me back, Cyrus would turn it all over. He would walk away from every bit of the system.

Tears pricked into my eyes. A sob tried to push its way over my lips, but the air couldn't move with his hand around my throat.

They both grinned wickedly.

"It has been building for centuries, lovely," he said. "And now, after all this time, we will finally make it happen. We will finally end the monarchy. And we will end Cyrus."

Tears slipped down my face, but steel framed its way around my heart.

I knew what that meant.

They would get Cyrus to give up the throne.

But then they would kill him.

They'd kill me.

They'd kill everyone at Court. And those who allied themselves with my son, those who wanted to take over the world, they would be in control.

So I waited.

I knew what I had to do.

It took so long until I had my opportunity. They kept me locked in a cell with nothing within reach. For days, probably weeks, we sailed toward Austria and the closest port.

But finally, I heard noise. I could smell something other than sea.

I climbed to my feet and waited for them to come retrieve me.

Roughly, they dragged me out of the cell and we went above deck. The moon shone brightly, illuminating the quiet but still-occupied port.

I walked down the plank, onto the dock. My eyes wildly searched, looking.

And there, just within my reach, I spotted a harpoon.

I moved faster than I'd ever moved.

I grabbed it.

And I buried it deep in my chest.

Pain seared through me, and then it pierced my heart.

I was dead. I would never make it back to Cyrus.

But without me, these men had nothing.

With me dead, he, and everyone at Court would remain safe.

And I knew, someday, I would be born again.

"WE MEET AGAIN, QUEEN SEVAN," THE MAN WITH THE SCAR says with a smug smile.

My movements invisible, I was so fast, I rush forward, wrapping my hand around his throat. His head cracks back against the wood studs.

"How many of you are there?" I hiss in his face. "Who else is here in Greendale?"

He just smiles, baring yellowed fangs. "This goes beyond the Born now," he says. "Others have not been happy with the reigning King, one who has had too much power for too long."

"Are you saying that some of the Royals are turning on Cyrus?" I demand, my grip on him tightening.

He just smiles and laughs.

I yank.

I rip his head clean from his shoulders and let it fall to the floor with a crack against the concrete.

My eyes dark and narrowed, I move over to the man who has gotten his front tooth replaced since the last time I saw him.

"Tell me everything you know," I growl.

His eyes narrow. "No."

My hand darts out and I grab one of his fingers, snapping it off.

The man screams out in pain.

"There are two factions trying to get Cyrus off the throne," I demand. "True or false?"

"There have always been those of us trying to get Cyrus

off the throne," the man growls through his pain. "Ever since he suppressed us. The time of humans must come to an end."

I snap another of his fingers off. "That is beside the point," I snarl. "The Born are trying to get to Cyrus through me. These Royals. Are they a real threat?"

The man smiles through his pain. It grows slowly.

"Oh how blind Cyrus has been to what has been going on within his own Court for so long. Cyrus cares about so little anymore. His focus has been on finding you, his long lost wife, for all these years. He didn't care to take note of the whisperings in his own land."

My blood rushes hot. But now fear races through my veins.

"Are the two groups working together?" I ask one more time.

The man laughs. "If we are, if we are not, either way, the King will fall now that you have returned."

My hand darts out and my fingers burrow into his chest as he lets out a choked off cry. Warm and wet, they know exactly where to search. The muscle and incredibly soft tissues pulse as my fingers wrap around it.

And I rip his heart out.

I stare at it, anger raging through me. Terror slips through my veins like a snake.

We've dealt with insurrection before. With assassination attempts.

But this one feels different. If what he said is true, if Royals are turning against us, the game will change.

"There are no others here, my Queen," Larkin speaks from the shadows. "I'm sure of it this time."

I nod, still staring at the man's heart.

"We are returning to Roter Himmel," I say as I squeeze the heart just a little tighter. "I'm taking my parents with me. I will bury them there. We can't leave any evidence here." My eyes flick up to Larkin's face. "Do you understand?"

"I do, my Queen," he says with a deep bow.

I turn, finding Ian standing there. Softly, I hear Alivia comforting Eshan upstairs.

"I need your help," I say to him, walking back toward the stairs.

Ian goes to steal a truck. There's no time to worry about renting one, not a second to be spared. He goes to the next neighborhood over and brings it back ten minutes later.

Larkin wrapped my parents' bodies in sheets. I'm ever grateful that I don't even have to see them.

I've dealt with dozens of bodies over the short course of my career as a mortician's assistant. I've cleaned gruesome things, washed plenty of blood.

It's different when it's your own parents. When it's the man who taught you how to drive, or the woman who put a bandage on your scraped knee.

I turn to Eshan, stone-faced before we leave.

"It's going to hit later," I say quietly to him. I look up into his beautiful face. He stares blankly at a streak of blood on the wood floor. "It's going to sink in later. And it's going to be bad. But right now we need to leave. I have to get back to Roter Himmel, to Cyrus."

He still doesn't look at me, so I place my hands on either side of his face, turning it to me. Finally, his eyes float to mine, and I see the terror in them.

"You're my brother," I say, my voice even. "Take away all of this stuff, every bit of it, and that's still true. You're my brother and we are family. And I am going to take care of you, Eshan. I promise."

His eyes clear just a bit as he understands what that means.

That I'm taking him with me to Roter Himmel. Taking him to stay, to live with me.

He looks scared, but he nods.

"Let's go," I say, wrapping an arm around him.

Together, Eshan, Ian, Alivia, and I climb into the truck. I slip into the backseat with my brother, and Ian drives us back to the airport.

I pull out my phone and touch the name on the screen.

"*Im yndmisht srtov*," Cyrus answers after only one ring.

"Cyrus," I say, and with his name, my emotional dam breaks open.

"What is it, my love?" he says, and I hear him whip into action. "Tell me where you are."

I squeeze my eyes closed, pushing out tears. "Cyrus, I have learned so much."

I can hear him storming through the castle, hear people scrambling to get out of his way, to do as he will demand.

"Talk to me," he says.

Another sob pushes out past my lips. "I remember it all, Cyrus. Everything." I take a deep breath in. "I knew there had been an eighth immortal death."

He's very quiet now, listening so intently.

"Cyrus, it has not been 286 years since I last died," I say as my stomach turns. "There was another life. As a descendant of the House of Himura. I tried to come to you. I was on my way."

A breath slips between Cyrus' lips.

I can only imagine how his heart is shattering.

It had been so long. Those 286 years are the longest we have ever been separated. The longest by far.

"Old ways of thinking are sparking to life again, *im yndmisht srtov*," I say. My voice trembles slightly, my voice going low. "They tried to use me to get to you. I stopped them then. I took matters into my own hands. They tried to get to me again, but we put a stop to it. But they are coming, Cyrus."

"Sevan," he breathes.

And finally, it doesn't hurt so much when he calls me that name.

"I'm on my way home," I say, looking out the window. We will be back at the airport in ten minutes. "Until I arrive, don't trust anyone. Not a soul."

"Sevan, I-"

But suddenly there is a loud, wet thwack sound. There's a loud clatter, as if the phone fell to the ground.

"Cyrus?" I call. My hands begin to tremble. "Cyrus?"

He doesn't answer.

I listen hard.

There's a sound, like something being dragged across a stone floor.

I hear a wet drip.

"Cyrus?" I breathe quietly. My entire body goes ice still. "Cyrus!" I scream.

The other line goes quiet for a second. And then muffled

noise. And then a quiet breath.

"It looks like we did not need you after all, Sevan," a voice says.

"What did you do?" I gasp.

The voice on the other end chuckles. "Oh, how the times will change."

"What did you do?" I scream.

I hear a shout on the phone, followed by another. The man on the other line makes a startled sound and a quick intake of breath.

More shouts.

Guards.

I can hear them.

Chaos.

"What did you do?" I scream again. "What have you done to Cyrus?"

But there's a loud cracking sound again, as if the phone was dropped once more, and the line goes dead.

I pull my phone away, staring at the screen, my mouth hanging open.

"What is it?" Alivia asks. "What happened?"

My mouth opens and closes. I shake my head. "I…I don't know. There was this man, and…"

A fog. A numbing fog takes over my brain.

I can't think.

I can't breathe.

I can't…

I can't…

"Drive faster," I grit out.

CHAPTER 35

It is the longest twelve hours in the long history of man and time.

A long flight on a jet. A drive from the airport through the familiar mountain pass. Circling around the lake I've always loved. Down a street that cuts through the village.

It's my home. But I don't see any of it.

And finally, finally, there rising before us, is the castle.

The home we built together. The place where we put in so many hours of hard, manual labor to make it livable.

We stop in front of the main gate and I climb out.

People stand to either side of the gate, every one of them bearing a solemn face. But as I look at them, I know they know.

They know exactly who I am.

The guards open the gates and without a second of hesitation, I walk in.

So many Royals line the way, creating a path through the castle. I do not have to ask where to find him, I do not have to ask where to go.

They lead a path straight to the great hall.

I stop when I step inside, my body going cold.

An iron cage sits in the middle of the room, holding a man who only stares at me with a smile.

I take a step forward, and then another step.

Beside the cage is a huge, long table. One that could seat fifty people.

Tears prick my eyes and my throat closes up.

My lips press together and tremble as I continue walking forward.

I stop beside the table, right in the center of it.

"Oh, how the times will change," the man in the cage says with a voice I will never forget.

Lying on the table is Cyrus.

My eyes rove over his powerful hands. Linger on his powerful forearms. Appreciate his strong chest.

A little tear comes to my eye when I see that incredibly thick hair. When I think of how those lips feel pressed to mine.

But a little scream slips over my lips.

There's blood.

Torn flesh.

I see bone.

Cyrus' body is perfectly still.

His head rests on the table, a foot separated from his shoulders.

"I am so sorry, my Queen," a guard says, kneeling before me. "He was decapitated by this man. The King…" the man's voice trembles, with horror, and fear. "The King is dead."

THE END OF BOOK TWO

ABOUT THE AUTHOR

 Keary Taylor is the USA TODAY best-selling author of over twenty novels. She grew up along the foothills of the Rocky Mountains where she started creating imaginary worlds and daring characters who always fell in love. She now splits her time between a tiny island in the Pacific Northwest and Utah, dragging along her husband and their two children. She continues to have an overactive imagination that frequently keeps her up at night.

To learn more about Keary, please visit her website: www.kearytaylor.com.

Made in the USA
Middletown, DE
11 April 2024

52917394R00165